ROBERT JORDAN

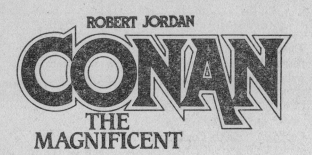

CONAN

THE
MAGNIFICENT

TOR

A TOM DOHERTY ASSOCIATES BOOK

CONAN THE MAGNIFICENT

First printing: May 1984
Fifth printing: January 1987

A TOR Book

Published by Tom Doherty Associates, Inc.
49 West 24 Street
New York, N.Y. 10010

Cover art by Boris Vallejo

ISBN: 0-812-54236-3
CAN. ED.: 0-812-54237-1

Printed in the United States of America

0 9 8 7 6 5

With a speed that seemed too great for its bulk, the glittering creature moved to within ten paces of the bound men. Suddenly the great, scaled head went back, and from its gaping maw came a shrill ululation that turned men's bones to water. Awed silence fell among the watchers, but one of the prisoners screamed, a high, thin sound with the reek of madness in it.

Mouth still open, the head lowered until those chill golden eyes regarded the captives. From those gaping jaws a gout of rubescent flame swept across the captives.

"*All praise to the true gods!*" the watchers cried.

"Death to the unbelievers!" The roar was deafening.

"*DEATH TO THE UNBELIEVERS!*"

"Although I have more than a mild prejudice against the sub-genre characterized by mighty thewed warriors pitted against ancient sorceries, I find that I actively look forward to each new Conan by Robert Jordan."

—*Science Fiction Chronicle*

Look for all these Conan books

CONAN THE DEFENDER
CONAN THE DESTROYER
CONAN THE FEARLESS
CONAN THE INVINCIBLE
CONAN THE MAGNIFICENT
CONAN THE RAIDER
CONAN THE RENEGADE
CONAN THE TRIUMPHANT
CONAN THE UNCONQUERED
CONAN THE VALOROUS
CONAN THE VICTORIOUS

CONAN
THE
MAGNIFICENT

WESTERN SEA

VANAHEIM

ASGAR

CIMMERIA

PICTISH WILDERNESS

MARCHES

BORDER KING

BOSSONIAN

GUNDERLAND

Velitrium

TAURAN

Galparan

Black R.

Shirki R.

Tanasul

NEMEDI

Thunder R.

AQUILONIA

Tarantia

Belverus

Numa

Shamar

Kordava

Almuric R.

Tyborg R.

Ianthe

OPHIR

ZINGARA

Red R.

Khorshemi

RABIRIAN MTS.

K

Khoraîas

ARGOS

BARACHA
ISLES

SHEM

Messantia

Eruk

Asgalun

River Styx

Khemi

Lux

STYGIA

SIPTAH'S
ISLE

Sukhmet

KUSH

DARFA

Xuthal

BLAC

Zarkheba R.

Xuch

CHAZAUD

CONAN
THE
MAGNIFICENT

PROLOGUE

Icy air hung deathly still among the crags of the Kezankian mountains, deep in the heart of that arm of those mountains which stretched south and west along the border between Zamora and Brythunia. No bird sang, and the cloudless azure sky was empty, for even the ever-present vultures could find no current on which to soar.

In that eerie quiesence a thousand fierce, turbanned Kezankian hillmen crowded steep brown slopes that formed a natural amphitheater. They waited and merged with the silence of the mountains. No sheathed tulwar clattered against stone. No booted foot shifted with the impatience that was plain on lean, bearded faces. They hardly seemed to breathe. Black eyes stared down unblinkingly at a space two hundred paces across, floored with great granite blocks and encircled by a waist-high wall as wide as a man was tall. Granite columns, thick and crudely hewn, lined the top of the wall like teeth in a sun-dried skull. In the center of that circle three men, pale-skinned Brythunians, were bound to tall stakes of black iron, arms stretched above their heads, leather cords digging cruelly into their wrists. But they were not the object of the watcher's attention. That was on the tall, scarlet-robed man with a forked beard who stood atop a tunnel of massive stone blocks that pierced the low wall and led back into the mountain behind him.

Basrakan Imalla, dark face thin and stern beneath a turban of red, green and gold, threw back his head and cried, "All glory be to the true gods!"

A sigh of exaltation passed through the watchers, and their response rumbled against the mountainsides. "All glory be to the true gods!"

Had Basrakan's nature been different, he might have smiled in satisfaction. Hillmen did not gather in large numbers, for every clan warred against every other clan, and the tribes were riddled by blood feuds. But he had gathered these and more. Nearly ten times their number camped amid the jagged mountains around the amphitheater, and scores of others joined them every day. With the power the true gods had given him, with the sign of their favor they had granted him, he had done what no other could. And he would do more! The ancient gods of the Kezankians had chosen him out.

"Men of the cities," he made the word sound obscene, "worship false gods! They know nothing of the true gods, the spirits of earth, of air, of water. And of fire!"

A wordless roar broke from a thousand throats,

approbation for Basrakan and hatred for the men of the cities melting together till even the men who shouted could not tell where one ended and the other began.

Basrakan's black eyes burned with fervor. Hundreds of Imallas wandered the mountains, carrying the word of the ancient gods from clan to clan, kept safe from feud and battle by the word they carried. But it had been given to him to bring about the old gods' triumph.

"The people of the cities are an iniquity in the sight of the true gods!" His voice rang like a deep bell, and he could feel his words resonate in the minds of his listeners. "Kings and lords who murder true believers in the names of the foul demons they call gods! Fat merchants who pile up more gold in their vaults than any clan of the mountains possesses! Princesses who flaunt their half-naked bodies and offer themselves to men like trulls! Trulls who drench themselves in perfumes and bedeck themselves in gold like princesses! Men with less pride than animals, begging in the streets! The filth of their lives stains the world, but we will wash it away in their blood!"

The scream that answered him, shaking the gray granite beneath his feet, barely touched his thoughts. Deep into the warren of caverns beneath this very mountain he had gone, through stygian passages lit only by the torch he carried, seeking to be closer to the spirits of the earth when he offered them prayers. There the true gods led him to the subterranean pool where eyeless, albescent fish swam around the clutch of huge eggs, as hard as the finest armor, left there countless centuries past.

For years he had feared the true gods would turn their faces from him for his study of the thaumaturgical arts, but only those studies had enabled him to transport the slick black spheres back to his hut. Without the knowledge from those studies he could never have succeeded in hatching one of the nine, could never have bound the creature that came from it to him, even as imperfectly as he had. If only he had the Eyes of Fire . . . no, *when* he had them all bonds, so tenuous now, would become as iron.

"We will kill the unbelievers and the defilers!" Basrakan intoned as the tumult faded. "We will tear down their cities and sow the ground whereon they stood with salt! Their women, who are vessels of lust, shall be scourged of their vileness! No trace of their blood shall remain! Not even a memory!" The hook-nosed Imalla threw his arms wide. "The sign of the true gods is with us!"

In a loud, clear voice he began to chant, each word echoing sharply from the mountains. The thousand watching warriors held their collective breath. He knew there were those listening who sought only gold looted from the cities rather than the purification of the world. Now they would learn to believe.

The last syllable of the incantation rang in the air like struck crystal. Basrakan ran his eyes over the Brythunian captives, survivors of a party of hunters who had entered the mountains from the west. One was no more than sixteen, his gray eyes twisted with fear, but the Imalla did not see the Brythunians as human. They were not of the tribes. They were outsiders. They were the sacrifice.

Basrakan felt the coming, a slow vibration of the stone beneath his feet, before he heard the rough scraping of claws longer than a man's hand.

"The sign of the true gods is with us!" he shouted again, and the creature's great head emerged from the tunnel.

A thousand throats answered the Imalla as the rest of the thick, tubular body came into view, more than fifteen paces in length and supported on four wide-set, massive legs. "The sign of the true gods is with us!" Awe and fear warred in that thunderous roar.

Blackened plates lined its short muzzle, overlapped by thick, irregular teeth designed for ripping flesh. The rest of that monstrous head and body were covered by scales of green and gold and scarlet, glittering in the pale sun, harder than the finest armor the hand of man could produce. On its back those scales had of late been displaced by two long, leathery boils. Drake, the ancient tomes called it, and if those volumes were correct about the hard, dull bulges, the sign of the true gods' favor would soon be complete.

The creature turned its head to stare with paralyzing intensity directly at Basrakan. The Imalla remained outwardly calm, but a core of ice formed in his stomach, and that coldness spread, freezing his breath and the words in his throat. That golden-eyed gaze always seemed to him filled with hatred. It could not be hatred of him, of course. He was blessed by the true gods. Yet the malevolence was there. Perhaps it was the contempt of a creature of the true gods for mere mortal men. In any case, the wards he had set between the crudely hewn granite columns would keep the drake within the circle, and the tunnel exited only there. Or did it? Though he had often descended into the caverns beneath the mountain—at least, in the days before he found the black drake eggs—he had not explored the tenth part of them. There could be a score of exits from that tangle of passages he had never found.

Those awesome eyes turned away, and Basrakan found himself drawing a deep breath. He was pleased to note there was no shudder in it. The favor of the old gods was truly with him.

With a speed that seemed too great for its bulk, the glittering creature moved to within ten paces of the bound men. Suddenly the great, scaled head went back, and from its gaping maw came a shrill ululation that froze men's marrow and turned their bones to water. Awed silence fell among the watchers, but one of the prisoners screamed, a high, thin sound with the reek of madness in it. The boy fought his cords silently; blood began to trickle down his arms.

The fiery-eyed Imalla brought his hands forward, palms up, as if offering the drake to the assemblage. "From the depths of the earth it comes!" he cried. "The spirits of earth are with us!"

Mouth still open, the drake's head lowered until those chill golden eyes regarded the captives. From those gaping jaws a gout of rubescent flame swept across the captives.

"Fire is its breath!" Basrakan shouted. "The spirits of fire are with us!"

Two of the prisoners were sagging torches, tunic and hair aflame. The youth, wracked with the pain of his burns, shrieked, "Mitra help me! Eldran, I—"

The iridescent creature took two quick paces forward, and a shorter burst of fire silenced the boy. Darting forward, the drake ripped a burning body in half. The crunching of bones sounded loudly, and gobbets of charred flesh dropped to the stone.

"The true gods are with us!" Basrakan declaimed. "On a day soon, the sign of the gods' favor will fly! The spirits of air are with us!" The old tomes had to be right, he thought. Those leathery bulges would burst, and wings would grow. They would! "On that day we will ride forth, invincible in the favor of the old gods, and purge the world with fire and steel! All praise be to the true gods!"

"*All praise be to the true gods*!" his followers answered.

"All glory to the true gods!"

"*All glory to the true gods*!"

"Death to the unbelievers!"

The roar was deafening. "*DEATH TO THE UN-BELIEVERS*!"

The thousand would stay to watch the feeding, for they were chosen by lot from the ever-growing number encamped in the surrounding mountains, and many had never seen it before. Basrakan had more impor tant matters to tend to. The drake would return to its caverns of its own accord when the bodies were consumed. The Imalla started up a path, well worn now in the brown stone by many journeys, that led from the amphitheater around the mountainside.

A man almost as tall as Basrakan and even leaner, his face burning with ascetic fanaticism above a plaited beard, met him and bowed deeply. "The blessings of the true gods be on you, Basrakan Imalla," the newcomer said. His turban of scarlet, green and gold marked him as Basrakan's acolyte, though his robe was of plain black. "The man Akkadan has come. I have had him taken to your dwelling."

No glimmer of Basrakan's excitement touched his stern face. The Eyes of Fire! He inclined his head slightly. "The blessings of the true gods be on you, Jbeil Imalla. I will see him now."

Jbeil bowed again; Basrakan went on, seemingly unhurried, but without even the inclination of his head this time.

The path led around the slope of the mountain to the village of stone houses, a score in number, that had grown up where once stood the hut in which Basrakan had lived. His followers had spoken of building a fortress for him, but he had no need of such. In time, though, he had allowed the construction of a dwelling for himself, of two stories and larger than all the rest of the village placed together. It was not a matter of pride, he often reminded himself, for he denied all pride save that of the old gods. The structure was for *their* glory.

Turbanned and bearded men in stained leather vests and voluminous trousers, the original color of which was a mystery lost in age and dirt, bowed as he passed, as did women covered from head to foot in black cloth, with only a slit for their eyes. He ignored them, as he did the two guards before his door, for he was openly hurrying now.

Within, another acolyte in multi-hued turban bent himself and gestured with a bony hand. "The blessings of the true gods be on you, Basrakan Imalla. The man Akkadan—"

"Yes, Ruhallah." Basrakan wasted not even moments on honorifics. "Leave me!" Without waiting to be obeyed, the tall Imalla swept through the door Ruhallah had indicated, into a room sparsely furnished with black-lacquered tables and stools. A hanging on one wall was a woven map of the nations from the Vilayet Sea west to Nemedia and Ophir.

Basrakan's face darkened at the sight of the man who waited there. Turban and forked beard proclaimed him hillman, but his fingers bore jeweled rings, his cloak was of purple silk and there was a plumpness about him that bespoke feasting and wine.

"You have spent too much time among the men of the cities, Akkadan," Basrakan said grimly. "No doubt you have partaken of their vices! Consorted with their women!"

The plump man's face paled beneath its swarthiness, and he quickly hid his beringed hands behind him as he bowed. "No, Basrakan Imalla, I have not. I swear!"

His words tumbled over each other in his haste. Sweat gleamed on his forehead. "I am a true—"

"Enough!" Basrakan spat. "You had best have what I sent you for, Akkadan. I commanded you not to return without the information."

"I have it, Basrakan Imalla. I have found them. And I have made plans of the palace and maps—"

Basrakan's shout cut him short. "Truly I am favored above all other men by the true gods!"

Turning his back on Akkadan, he strode to the wall hanging, clenched fists raised in triumph toward the nations represented there. Soon the Eyes of Fire would be his, and the drake would be bound to him as if part of his flesh and will. And with the sign of the true gods' favor flying before his followers, no army of mortal men would long stand against them.

"All glory to the true gods," Basrakan whispered fiercely. "Death to all unbelievers!"

Chapter 1

Night caressed Shadizar, that city known as 'the Wicked,' and veiled the happenings which justified that name a thousand times over. The darkness that brought respite to other cities drew out the worst in Shadizar of the Alabaster Towers, Shadizar of the Golden Domes, city of venality and debauchery.

In a score of marble chambers silk-clad nobles coerced wives not theirs to their beds, and many-chinned merchants licked fat lips over the abductions of competitors' nubile daughters. Perfumed wives, fanned by slaves wielding snowy ostrich plumes, plotted the cuckolding of husbands, sometimes their own, while hot-eyed young women of wealth or noble birth or both schemed at circumventing the guards placed on their supposed chastity. Nine women and thirty-one men, one a beggar and one a lord, died by murder. The gold of ten wealthy men was taken from iron vaults by thieves, and fifty others increased their wealth at the expense of the poor. In three brothels perversions never before contemplated by humankind were created. Doxies beyond numbering plied their ancient trade from the shadows, and twisted, ragged beggars preyed on the trulls' wine-soaked patrons. No man walked the streets unarmed, but even in the best quarters of the city arms were often not enough to save one's silver from cutpurses and footpads. Night in Shadizar was in full cry.

Wisps of cloud, stirred by a warm breeze, dappled the moon sitting high in the sky. Vagrant shadows fled over the rooftops, yet they were enough for the massively muscled young man, swordbelt slung across his broad chest so that the worn hilt of his broadsword projected above his right shoulder, who raced with them from chimney to chimney. With a skill born in the savage wastes of his native Cimmerian mountains he blended with the drifting shades, and was invisible to the eyes of the city-born.

The roof the muscular youth traveled came to an end, and he peered down into the blackness hiding the paving stones of the street, four stories below. His eyes were frozen sapphires, and his face, a square-cut lion's mane of black held back from it by a leather cord, showed several ordinary lifetimes' experience despite its youth. He eyed the next building, an alabaster cube with a freize of scrollwork running all the way around it an arm's length below the roof. From deep in his throat came a soft growl. A good six paces wide, the street was, although it was the narrowest of the four that surrounded the nearly palatial structure. What he had not noticed when he chose this approach—eying the distances from the ground—was that the far roof was sloped. Steeply! Erlik take Baratses, he thought. And his gold!

This was no theft of his own choosing, but rather was at the behest of the merchant Baratses, a purveyor of spices from the most distant realms of the world. Ten pieces of gold the spice dealer had offered for the most prized possession of Samarides, a wealthy importer of gems: a goblet carved from a single huge emerald. Ten pieces of gold was the hundredth part of the goblet's worth, one tenth of what the fences in the Desert would pay, but a run of bad luck with the dice had put the Cimmerian in urgent need of coin. He had agreed to theft and price, and taken two gold pieces in advance, before he even knew what was to be stolen. Still, a bargain sworn to must be kept. At least, he thought grimly, there was no guard atop the other building, as there were on so many other merchants' roofs.

"Crom!" he muttered with a last look at Samarides' roof, and moved back from the edge, well back into the shadows among the chimneys. Breathing deeply to charge his lungs, he crouched. His eyes strained toward the distant rooftop. Suddenly, like a hunting leopard, he sprang forward; in two strides he was sprinting at full speed. His lead foot touched the edge of the roof, and he leaped, hurling himself into the air with arms outstretched, fingers curled to grab. With a crash he landed at full length on the sloping roof. And immediately began to slide. Desperately he spread his arms and legs to slow himself; his eyes searched for a projection to grasp, for the smallest nub that might stop his fall. Inexorably he moved toward the drop to the pavement.

No wonder there was no watchman on the roof, he thought, furious at himself for not questioning that lack earlier. The rooftiles were glazed to a surface like oiled porcelain. In the space of a breath his feet were over the edge, then his legs. Abruptly his left hand slid into a gap where a tile was missing. Tiles shattered as his weight smashed his vainly gripping hand through them; fragments showered past him into the gloom beneath. Wood slapped his palm; convulsively he clutched. With a jerk that wrenched at the heavy muscles of his shoulder he was brought up short to swing over the shadowed four-story drop.

For the first time since his leap he made a sound, a long, slow exhalation between his teeth. "Ten gold pieces," he said in a flat voice, "are not enough."

Suddenly the wooden roof-frame he was grasping gave with a sharp snap, and he was falling again. Twisting as he dropped, he stretched, caught the finger-joint-wide ledge at the bottom of the frieze by his fingertips, and slammed flat against the alabaster wall.

"Not nearly enough," he panted when he had regained his breath. "I've half a mind to take the accursed thing to Zeno after this." But even as he said it he knew he would not go to the Nemedian fence. He had given his word.

At the moment, he realized, his problem lay not in how to dispose of the emerald goblet, but in how to leave his present position with a whole skin. The only openings piercing the alabaster wall at this height were ventilation holes the size of his fist, for the top floor and the attic were given over to storage and quarters for servants and slaves. Such needed no windows, to the mind of Samarides, and if they had them would only lean out and spoil the appearance of his fine house. No other ledges or friezes broke the smoothness of the walls, nor were there balconies overlooking the street. The roof he had first leaped from might as well have been in Sultanapur, the roof above as well have been beyond the clouds. That, the dangling youth reluctantly concluded, left only the windows of the third floor, their arched tops a good armspan lower than his feet.

It was not his way to dally when his course was decided. Slowly, hanging by his fingertips, he worked his way along the narrow ledge. The first two arched windows to pass beneath his feet glowed with light. He could not risk meeting people. The third, however, was dark.

Taking a deep breath, he let go his hold and dropped, his body brushing lightly against the wall. If he touched the wall too much, it would push him out and away to fall helplessly. As he felt his legs come in front of the window, he moved his feet inward, toward the window sill. Stone smashed against his soles, his palms slapped hard against the sides of the window, and he hung precariously, leaning outward. The thickness of the wall, the depth of the window, denied even a fingernail's hold. Only the outward pressure of his hands kept him from hurtling to the street.

Muscles knotted with the strain, he drew himself forward until he could step within Samarides' dwelling. As his foot touched the carpet-strewn floor, his hand went to the worn leather of his sword hilt. The room was dark, yet his night-accustomed eyes could make out the dim shapes of cushioned chairs. Tapestries, their colors reduced to shadings of gray, hung on the walls, and a dimly patterned carpet covered the marble floor. With a sigh he relaxed, a trifle, at least. This was no sleeping chamber, with someone to awaken and scream an alarm. It was about time something went right on this night of continuous near-disaster.

There were still problems, though. He was unsure whether the worst of these was how to get out of the dwelling—or how to get to his goal. Samarides' house was arranged around a central garden, where the gem merchant spent a great deal of his time among the fountains. The only door of the room in which he displayed his treasures opened onto the ground-floor colonnade around that garden.

It would have been easy to climb down from the roof to the garden, and Baratses had told him exactly the location of the door to the treasure room. Now he must make his way through the corridors, and risk coming on servants or guards.

Opening the door a crack, he peered into the hall, lit by gilded brass oil lamps hung on chains from bronze wall sconces. Tables inlaid with mother-of-pearl stood at intervals along walls mosaicked in intricate patterns with thousands of tiny, multihued tiles. No one trod the polished marble floor. Silently he slipped into the corridor.

For a heartbeat he stood, picturing the plan of the house in his mind. The treasure room was in *that* direction. Ears straining for the slightest hint of another's footstep, he hurried through the halls with a tread as light as a cat. Back stairs led downward, then others took him down again. Their location and the fact that their dark red tiles were dull and worn marked them as servant's stairs. Twice the scuff of sandals from a crossing corridor gave warning, and he pressed his back to a wall, barely breathing, while unseeing servants in pale blue tunics scurried by, too intent on their labors to so much as glance down the branching way.

Then he was into the central garden, the high, shadowed walls of the house making it a small canyon. Splash and burble echoed softly from half-a-score fountains, scattered among fig trees and flowering plants and alabaster statuary. The treasure room lay directly opposite him across the garden.

He took a step, and froze. A dim shape hurried toward him down one of the garden paths. Silently he moved further to the side, away from the light spilling from the doorway. The approaching figure slowed. Had he been seen, he wondered. Whoever was coming moved very slowly, now, seeming almost to creep, and made no sound at all. Abruptly the figure left the slated walk and moved toward him again. His jaw tightened; no other muscle of him moved, not so much as an eyelid blinking. Closer. Ten paces. Five. Two.

Suddenly the strangely still-dim figure froze, gasped. The big youth sprang. One hand cut off sound by covering the mouth that uttered it. His other arm pinned the figure's arms. Teeth dug into his calloused palm, and his captive flung about wildly, kicks thudding against his legs.

"Erlik take you!" he hissed. "You fight like a woman! Stop that, and I'll not hurt—"

It penetrated his mind that the body he held was rounded, if firm. He side-stepped to the edge of the light from the doorway, and found himself studying large, brown eyes that were suddenly frowning above his hand. It *was* a woman, and a pretty one, with satiny, olive skin and her hair braided tightly about her small head. The biting stopped, and he loosed his grip on her jaw. He opened his mouth to say he would not harm her if she gave no outcry, but she cut him off.

"I am a sorcereress," she whispered hoarsely, "and I know you, Conan, far-traveler from Samaria, or Cymria, or some such place. You think you are a thief. Release me!"

The hairs on the back of his neck stirred. How

could she know? He seemed to have a talent for running afoul of sorcerers, a talent he would just as soon lose. His grip was loosening when he became aware of the amused gleam in her big eyes, and the way her small, white teeth were biting a full lower lip. For the first time he took in her garb, snug, dull black from neck to toes. Even her feet were covered in ebon cloth, with the big toe separated like the thumb on a mitten.

Holding her out from him by her upper arms, he was unable to suppress a smile. Slender, she was, and short, but the close fit of her odd garments left no doubts as to her womanhood. She kicked at him, and he caught it on his thigh.

"Sorcereress?" he growled softly. "Then why do I think you'll change your story should I take a switch to your rump?"

"Why do I think that at the first blow I'll howl loudly enough to bring half the city?" she whispered back. "But truly I don't wish to. My name is Lyana, and I've heard of you, Conan. I've seen you in the streets. And admired you. I just wanted to sound mysterious, so I could compete with your other women." She shifted in his grasp, and her round breasts, large on her diminutive slimness, seemed even more prominent. Her tongue wet her lips, and she smiled invitingly. "Could you please put me down? You're so strong, and you're hurting me."

He hesitated, then lowered her feet to the ground. "What is this garb you wear, Lyana?"

"Forget that," she breathed, swaying closer. "Kiss me."

Despite himself his hands came up to clasp her face. Before his fingers touched her cheeks, she dropped to her knees and threw herself into a forward tumble past him. Stunned, he still managed to whirl after her. One tiny foot flashing from the middle of her roll caught him under the ribs, bringing a grunt, slowing him enough for her to come to her feet facing the wall . . . and she seemed to go up it like a spider.

With an oath Conan leaped forward. Something struck his arm, and he grabbed a soft, black-dye rope, hanging from above.

"Mitra blast me for a fool!" he grated. "A thief!"

Soft laughter floated down from close enough over his head to make him peer sharply upwards. "You are a fool." The girl's soft tones brimmed with mirth. "And I am indeed a thief, which you'll never be. Perhaps, with those shoulders, you could be a carter. Or a cart horse."

Snarling, Conan took hold of the rope to climb. A flicker caught the corner of his eye, and he felt more than heard something strike the ground by his foot. Instinctively, he jumped back, losing his grip on the rope. His grab to regain it brushed only the free end as it was drawn up.

"It would have struck you," the girl's low voice came again, "had I intended it so. Were I you, I'd leave here. Now. Fare you well, Conan."

"Lyana?" he whispered roughly. "Lyana?" Mocking silence answered him.

Muttering under his breath, he searched the ground around his feet, and tugged a flat, black throwing knife from the dirt. He tucked it behind his swordbelt, then stiffened as if stabbed.

The girl was a thief, and she had come from the direction of the treasure room. Cursing under his breath he ran, heedless of the rare shrubs and plants he passed.

An arched door led into the chamber where Samarides kept his most valuable possessions, and that door stood open. Conan paused a moment to study the heavy iron lock. That the girl had opened it he had no doubt, but if she had been within, then any traps must have been disabled, or else be easily avoided.

The Cimmerian hesitated a moment longer, then started across the chamber, floored in diamond-shaped tiles of alternating red and white. The emerald goblet, he had been told, stood at the far end of the room on a pedestal carved of serpentine. At his second step a diamond tile sank beneath his foot. Thinking of crossbows mounted on the wall—he had encountered such before—he threw himself flat on the floor. And felt another tile sink beneath his hand. From the wall came a rattling clink and clatter he had been a thief long enough to recognize. The sinking tiles had each released a weight which was pulling a chain from a wheel. And that in turn would activate . . . what?

As he leaped to his feet a bell began to toll, then another. Cursing, he ran the length of the room. Twice more tiles sank beneath him, and by the time he reached the dull green mottled pedestal, four bells clanged the alarm. The pedestal was bare.

"Erlik take the wench!" he snarled.

Spinning, he dashed from the chamber. And ran head-on into two spear-carrying guards. As the three fell to the floor it flashed into Conan's head that it was just as well he had not dallied to choose something to make up for the loss of the goblet. His fist smashed into the face of one guard, nose and teeth cracking in a spray of red. The man jerked and sagged, unconscious. The other scrambled to his feet, spear ready to thrust. Had he delayed, Conan thought, they could likely have held him in the chamber long enough for others to arrive. His sword flickered from its sheath, caught the spear just behind the head, and the second guard found himself holding a long stick. With a shout the man threw the pole at Conan and fled.

Conan ran, too. In the opposite direction. At the first doorway of the house he ducked inside, bursting into the midst of servants nervously chattering about the still ringing bells. For an instant they stared at him, eyes going wider and wider, then he waved his sword in the air and roared at the top of his lungs. Shrieking men and women scattered like a covey of Kothian quail.

Confusion, the Cimmerian thought. If he spread enough confusion he might get out of there yet.

Through the house he sped, and every servant he met was sent flying by fierce roars and waving blade, till cries of "Help!" and "Murder!" and even "Fire!" rang down every corridor. More than once the young Cimmerian had to duck down a side hall as guards clattered by, chasing after screams and yelling themselves, until he began to wonder how many men Samarides had. Cacophony run riot filled the house.

At last he reached the entry hall, surrounded on three sides by a balcony with balustrades of smoke-stone, beneath a vaulted ceiling worked in alabaster arabesques. Twin broad stairs of black marble curved down from that second-floor balcony to a floor mosa-icked in a map of the world, as Zamorans knew it, with each country marked by representations of the gems imported from it.

All of this Conan ignored, his eyes locked on the tall, iron-studded doors leading to the street. A bar, heavy enough to need three men for the lifting, held them shut, and the bar was in turn fastened in place by iron chains and massive locks.

"Crom!" he growled. "Shut up like a fortress!"

Once, twice, thrice his broadsword clashed against a lock, with him wincing at the damage the blows were doing to his edge. The lock broke open, and he quickly pulled the chain through the iron loops hold-ing it against the bar. As he turned to the next chain, a quarrel as thick as two of his fingers slammed into the bar where he had been standing. He changed his turn into a dive to the floor, eyes searching for the next shot.

Instantly he saw his lone opponent. Atop one flight of stairs stood a man of immense girth, whose skin yet hung in folds as if he had once been twice so big. Lank, thinning hair surrounded his puffy face, and he wore a shapeless sleeping garment of dark blue silk. Samarides. One of the gem merchant's feet was in the stirrup of a heavy crossbow, and he laboriously worked the handles of a windlass to crank back the bowstring, a rope of drool running from one corner of his narrow mouth.

Quickly judging how long it would be before Samarides could place another quarrel in the crossbow, Conan bounded to his feet. A single furious blow that struck sparks sent the second lock clattering to the floor. Sheathing his sword, the Cimmerian tugged the chain free and set his hands to the massive bar.

"Guards!" Samarides screamed. "To me! Guards!"

Muscles corded and knotted in calves and thighs, back, shoulders and arms, as Conan strained against the huge wooden bar. By the thickness of a fingernail it lifted. Sweat popped out on his forehead. The thickness of a finger. The width of a hand. And then the massive bar was clear of the support irons.

Three slow, staggering steps backwards Conan took, until he could turn and heave the bar aside. Mosaic tiles shattered as it landed with a crash that shook the floor.

"Guards!" Samarides shrieked, and pounding feet answered him.

Conan dashed to the thick, iron-studded doors and

heaved one open to crash against a wall. As he darted through, another quarrel slashed past his head to gouge a furrow in the marble of Samarides' portico. Tumult rose behind him as guards rushed into the entry hall, shouting to Samarides for instructions, and Samarides screamed incoherently back at them. Conan did not look back. He ran. Mind filled with anger at a young woman thief with a too-witty tongue, he ran until the night of Shadizar swallowed him.

Chapter 2

That quarter of Shadizar called the Desert was a warren of crooked steets reeking of offal and despair. The debaucheries that took place behind closed doors in the rest of the city were performed openly in the Desert, and made to pay a profit. Its denizens, more often in rags than not, lived as if death could come with the next breath, as it quite often did. Men and women were scavengers, predators or prey, and some who thought themselves in one class discovered, frequently too late, that they were in another.

The tavern of Abuletes was one of the Desert's best, as such was accounted there. Few footpads and fewer cutpurses were numbered among its patrons. Graverobbers were unwelcome, though more for the smells that hung about them than for how they earned their coin. For the rest, all who had the price of a drink were welcome.

When Conan slapped open the tavern door, the effluvia of the street fought momentarily with the smell of half-burned meat and sour wine in the big common room where two musicians playing zithers for a naked dancing girl competed unsuccessfully with the babble of the tavern's custom. A mustachioed Nemedian coiner at the bar fondled a giggling doxy in a tall, red-dyed wig and strips of green silk that did little to cover her generously rounded breasts and buttocks. A plump Ophirean procurer, jeweled rings glittering on his fingers, held court at a corner table; among those laughing at his jokes—so long as his gold held out, at least—were three kidnappers, swarthy, narrow-faced Iranistanis, hoping he would throw a little business their way. A pair of doxies, dark-eyed twins, hawked their wares among the tables, their girdles of coins clinking as their hips swayed in unison.

Before the Cimmerian had taken a full step, a voluptuous, olive-skinned woman threw her arms around his neck. Gilded brass breastplates barely contained her heavy breasts, and a narrow girdle of gilded chain, set low on her well-rounded hips, supported a length of diaphanous blue silk, no more than a handspan in width, that hung to her braceleted ankles before and behind.

"Ah, Conan," she murmured thoatily, "what a pity you did not return earlier."

"Have some wine with me, Semiramis," he replied, eying her swelling chest, "and tell me why I should have come back sooner. Then we can go upstairs—" He cut off with a frown as she shook her head.

"I ply my trade this night, Cimmerian." At his

frown, she sighed. "Even I must have a little silver to live."

"I have silver," he growled.

"And I cannot take coin from you. I will not."

He muttered an oath under his breath. "You always say that. Why not? I don't understand."

"Because you're not a woman." She laughed softly and traced a finger along his jaw. "A thing for which I am continually grateful."

Conan's face tightened. First Lyana had made a fool of him this night, and now Semiramis attempted the same. "Women never say their minds straight out. Very well. If you've no use for me tonight, then I'm done with you as well." He left her standing with her fists on her hips and her mouth twisted in exasperation.

At the bar he dug into his purse and tossed coppers onto the cracked wooden surface. As he had known it would, the sound of coins penetrated the wall of noise in the room and drew Abuletes, wiping his fat fingers on the filthy apron he wore over a faded yellow tunic. The tavernkeeper made the coins disappear with a deft motion.

"I want wine for that," Conan said. Abuletes nodded. "And some information."

" 'Tis enough for the wine," the tavernkeeper replied drily. He set a wooden tankard, from which rose the sour smell of cheap wine, before the big youth. "Information costs more."

Conan rubbed his thumb over a gouge in the edge of the bar, made by a sword stroke, drawing the fat man's piggish eyes to the mark. "There were six of them, as I recall," he said absently. "One with his knife pricking your ribs, and ready to probe your guts if you opened your mouth without his leave. What was it they intended? Taking you into the kitchen, wasn't it? Didn't one of them speak of putting your feet in the cookfire till you told where your gold is cached?"

"I have no gold," Abuletes muttered unconvincingly. He could spot a clipped coin at ten paces, and was reliably rumored to have the first copper he had ever stolen buried somewhere in the tavern.

"Of course not," Conan agreed smoothly. "Still, it was Hannuman's own luck for you I saw what was happening, when none else did. 'Twould have been . . . uncomfortable for you, with your feet in the coals and naught to tell them."

"Aye, you saw." The fat man's tone was as sour as his wine. "And laid about you with that accursed sword, splintering half my tables. Do you know what they cost to replace? The doxies were hysterical for all the blood you splattered around, and half my night's custom disappeared for fear you'd cut them down as well."

Conan laughed and drank deeply from the tankard, saying no more. Never a night passed without blood shed on the sawdust-strewn floor, and it was no rare sight to see a corpse being dragged out back for disposal in an alley.

Abuletes' face twisted, and his chin sank until his

chins doubled in number. "This makes it clear between us. Right?"

The Cimerian nodded, but cautioned, "If you tell me what I want to hear. I look for a woman." Abuletes snorted and gestured to the doxies scattered through the common room. Conan went on patiently. "She's a thief, about so tall," he marked with one big hand at the height of his chest, "and well rounded for her size. Tonight she wore black leggings and a short tunic, both as tight as her skin. And she carried this." He laid the thowing knife on the bar. "She calls herself Lyana."

Abuletes prodded the black blade with a grimy-knuckled finger. "I know of no woman thief, called Lyana or aught else. There was a man, though, who used knives like this. Jamal, he was named."

"A woman, Abuletes."

The fat tapster shrugged. "He had a daughter. What was her name? Let me see." He rubbed at a suety cheek. "Jamal was shortened a head by the City Guard, it must be ten years back. His brothers took the girl in. Gayan and Hafid. They were thieves, too. Haven't heard of them in years, though. Too old for the life now, I suppose. Age gets us all, in the end. Tamira. That was her name. Tamira."

The muscular youth stared expressionless at Abuletes until the fat tavernkeeper fell silent. "I ask about a girl called Lyana, and you spin me a tale of this Tamira. And her entire Mitra-accursed family. Would you care to tell me about her mother? Her grandfather? I've a mind to put your feet in the fire myself."

Abuletes eyed Conan warily. The man with the strange blue eyes was known in the Desert for his sudden temper, and for his unpredictability. The tavernkeeper spread his hands. "How hard is it to give a name not your own? And didn't I say? Jamal and his brothers wore the black garments you spoke of. Claimed it made them all but invisible in the dark. Had all sorts of tricks, they did. Ropes of raw silk dyed black, and I don't know what all. No, Tamira's your female thief, all right, whatever she calls herself now."

Black ropes, Conan thought, and suppressed a smile. Despite his youth he had had enough years as a thief to learn discretion. "Perhaps," was all he said.

"Perhaps," the tapster grumbled. "You mark me on it. She's the one. This makes us even, Cimmerian."

Conan finished his wine in three long gulps and set the empty tankard down with a click. "If she *is* the woman I seek. The question now is where to find her and make certain."

Abuletes threw up his pudgy hands. "Do you think I keep track of every woman in the Desert? I can't even keep track of the trulls in my own tavern!"

Conan turned his back on the tavernkeeper's grinding teeth. Tamira and Lyana, he was sure, were one and the same woman. Luck must be with him, for he had expected days of asking to find a trace of her. Denizens of the Desert left as few tracks as the animals of that district's namesake. Surely discovering so much so quickly was an omen. No doubt he would leave the tavern in the morning and find her walking past in the street. Then they would see who would make a fool of whom.

At that moment his eye fell on Semiramis, seated at a table with three Kothian smugglers. One, with his mustache curled like horns and big gilded hoops in his ears, kneaded her bare thigh as he spoke to her urgently. Nodding in sudden decision, Conan strode to the table where the four sat.

The Kothians looked up, and Semiramis frowned. "Conan," she began, reaching toward him cautioningly.

The big Cimmerian grasped her wrist, bent and, before anyone could move, hoisted her over his shoulder. Stools crashed over as the Kothians leaped to their feet, hands going to sword hilts.

"You northland oaf!" Semiramis howled, wriggling furiously. Her fist pounded futilely at his back. "Unhand me, you misbegotten spawn of a camel! Mitra blast your eyes, Conan!"

Her tirade went on, getting more inventive, and Conan paused to listen admiringly. The Kothians hesitated with swords half drawn, disconcerted at being ignored. After a moment Conan turned his attention to them, putting a pleasant smile on his face. That seemed to unsettle the three even more.

"My sister," he said mildly. "She and I must speak of family matters."

"Erlik flay your hide and stake your carcass in the sun!" the struggling woman yelled. "Derketo shrivel your stones!"

Calmly Conan met each man's gaze in turn, and each man shivered, for his smile did not extend to those glacial blue orbs. The Kothians measured the breadth of his shoulders, calculated how encumbered he would be by the woman, and tossed the dice in the privacy of their minds.

"I wouldn't interfere between brother and sister," the one with hoops in his ears muttered, his eyes sliding away. Suddenly all three were engrossed in setting their stools upright.

Semiramis' shouts redoubled in fury as Conan started for the rickety stairs that led to the second floor. He smacked a rounded buttock with his open palm. "Your sweet poetry leads me to believe you love me," he said, "but your dulcet tones would deafen an ox. Be quiet."

Her body quivered. It took him a moment to realize she was laughing. "Will you at least let me walk, you untutored beast?" she asked.

"No," he replied with a grin.

"Barbarian!" she murmured, and snuggled her cheek against his back.

Laughing, he took the stairs two at a time. Luck was indeed with him.

Chapter 3

The Katara Bazaar was a kaleidoscope of colors and a cacophony of voices, a large, flagstone-paved square near the Desert where sleek lordlings, perfumed pomanders at their nostrils, rubbed shoulders with unwashed apprentices who apologized with mocking grins when they jostled the well-born. Silk-clad ladies, trailed by attentive slaves to carry their purchases, browsed unmindful of the ragged urchins scurrying about their feet. Some vendors displayed their goods on flimsy tables sheltered by faded lengths of cloth on poles. Others had no more than a blanket spread beneath the hot sun. Hawkers of plums and ribbons, oranges and pins, cried their wares shrilly as they strolled through the throng. Rainbow bolts of cloth, carved ivories from Vendhya, brass bowls from Shadizar's own metalworkers, lustrous pearls from the Western Sea and paste "gems" guaranteed to be genuine, all changed hands in the space of a heartbeat. Some were stolen, some smuggled. A rare few had even had the King's tax paid on them.

On the morning after his attempt at Samarides' goblet—the thought made him wince—Conan made his way around the perimeter of the bazaar, searching without seeming to among the beggars. Mendicants were not allowed within the confines of the great square, but they lined its edges, their thin, supplicating cries entreating passersby for a coin. There was a space between each ragged man and the next, and unlike beggars elsewhere in Shadizar these cooperated to the extent of maintaining that distance. Too many too close together would reduce each man's take.

Exchanging a copper with a fruitmonger for two oranges, the big Cimmerian squatted near a beggar in filthy rags, a man with one leg twisted grotesquely at the knee. A grimy strip of cloth covered his eyes, and a wooden bowl with a single copper in the bottom sat on the flagstones before him.

"Pity the blind," the beggar whined loudly. "A coin for the blind, gentle people. Pity the blind."

Conan tossed one orange into the bowl and began stripping the peel from the other. "Ever think of going back to being a thief, Peor?" he said quietly.

The "blind" man turned his head sightly to make sure no one else was close by and said, "Never, Cimmerian." His cheerful voice was pitched to reach Conan's ear and no further. He made the orange disappear beneath his tunic of patches. "For later. No, I pay my tithe to the City Guard, and I sleep easy at night knowing my head will never go up on a pike over the West Gate. You should consider becoming a beggar. 'Tis a solid trade. Not like thieving. Mitra-accursed mountain slime!''

Conan paused with a segment of orange half-lifted to his mouth. "What?"

Barely moving his head, Peor motioned to a knot of six Kezankian hillmen, turbanned and bearded, their dark eyes wide with ill-concealed amazement at the city around them. They wandered through the bazaar in a daze, fingering goods but never buying. From the scowls that followed them, the peddlers were glad to see their backs, sale or no. "That's the third lot of those filthy jackals I've seen today, and a good two turns of the glass till the sun is high. They should be running for the rocks they crawled out from under, what with the news that's about this morning."

The beggar got little chance between sunrise and sunset to say anything beyond his pleading cry, and the occasional fawning thanks. It could not hurt to let him talk, Conan thought, and said, "What news?"

Peor snorted. "If it was about a new method of winning at dice, Cimmerian, you'd have known of it yesterday. Do you think of anything but women and gambling?"

"The news, Peor?"

"They say someone is uniting the Kezankian tribes. They say the hillmen are sharpening their tulwars. They say it could mean war. If 'tis so, the Desert will feel the first blow, as always."

Conan tossed the last of the orange aside and

wiped his hands on his thighs. "The Kezankians are far distant, Peor." His grin revealed strong white teeth. "Or do you think the tribesmen will leave their mountains to sack the Desert? It is not the place I would chose, were I they, but you are older than I and no doubt know better."

"Laugh, Cimmerian," Peor said bitterly. "But when war is announced the mob will hunt for hillman throats to slit, and when they cannot find enough to sate their bloodlust, they'll turn their attentions to the Desert. And the army will be there—'to preserve order.' Which means to put to the sword any poor sod from the Desert who thinks of actually resisting the mob. It has happened before, and will again."

A shadow fell across them, cast by a woman whose soft robes of emerald silk clung to the curves of breasts and belly and thighs like a caress. A belt woven of golden cords was about her waist. Ropes of pearls encircled her wrists and neck, and two more, as large as a man's thumbnail, were at her ears. Behind her a tall Shemite, the iron collar of a slave on his neck and a bored expression on his face, stood laden with packages from the Bazaar. She dropped a silver coin in Peor's bowl, but her sultry gaze was all for Conan.

The muscular youth enjoyed the looks women gave him, as a normal matter, but this one examined him as if he were a horse in the auction barns. And to make matters worse a scowl grew on the Shemite's face as though he recognized a rival. Conan's face grew hot with anger. He opened his mouth, but she spoke first.

"My husband would never approve the purchase," she smiled, and walked away with undulating hips. The Shemite hurried after her, casting a self-satisfied glance over his shoulder at Conan as he went.

Peor's bony fingers fished the coin from the bowl. With a cackle that showed he had regained at least some of his humor, he tucked it into his pouch. "And she'd pay a hundred times so much for a single night with you, Cimmerian. Two hundred. A more pleasant way to earn your coin than scrambling over rooftops, eh?"

"Would you like that leg broken in truth?" Conan growled.

The beggar's cackles grew until they took him into a fit of coughing. When he could breathe normally again, he wiped the back of his hand across his thin-lipped mouth. "No doubt I would earn even more in my bowl. My knee hurts of a night for leaving it so all day, but that fall was the best thing that ever happened to me."

Conan shivered at the thought, but pressed on while the other held his good mood. "I did not come today just to give you an orange, Peor. I look for a woman called Lyana, or perhaps Tamira."

Peor nodded as the Cimmerian described the girl and gave a carefully edited account of their meeting, then said, "Tamira. I've heard that name, and seen the girl. She looks as you say."

"Where can I find her?" Conan asked eagerly, but the beggar shook his head.

"I said I've seen her, and more than once, but as to where she might be. . . ." He shrugged.

Conan put a hand to the leather purse at his belt. "Peor, I could manage a pair of silver pieces for the man who tells me how to find her."

"I wish I knew," Peor said ruefully, then went on quickly. "But I'll pass the word among the Brotherhood of the Bowl. If a beggar sees her, you'll hear of it. After all, friendship counts for something, does it not?"

The Cimmerian cleared his throat to hide a grin. Friendship, indeed! The message would come to him through Peor, and the beggar who sent it would be lucky to get as much as one of the silver pieces. "That it does," he agreed.

"But, Conan? I don't hold with killing women. You don't intend to hurt her, do you?"

"Only her pride," Conan said, getting to his feet. With the beggars' eyes as his, he would have her before the day was out. "Only her pride."

Two days later Conan threaded his way through the thronging crowds with a sour expression on his face. Not only the beggars of Shadizar had become his eyes. More than one doxy had smiled at the ruggedly handsome young Cimmerian, shivered in her depths at the blue of his eyes, and promised to watch for the woman he sought, though never without a pout of sultry jealousy. The street urchins, unimpressed by broad shoulders or azure eyes, had been more difficult. Some men called them the Dust, those homeless, ragged children, countless in number and helpless before the winds of fate, but the streets of Shadizar were a hard school, and the urchins gave trust grudgingly and demanded a reward in silver. But from all those eyes he had learned only where Tamira had been, and never a word of where she was.

Conan's eyes searched among the passersby, seeking to pierce the veils of those women who wore them. At least, the veils of those who were slender and no taller than his chest. What he would do when he found her was not yet clear in his mind beyond the matter of seeking restitution for his youthful pride, but find her he would if he had to stare into the face of every woman in Shadizar.

So intent was he on his thoughts that the drum that cleared others from the street, even driving sedan chairs to the edge of the pavement, did not register on his mind until it suddenly came to him that he stood alone in the middle of the street. Turning to see where the steady thump came from, he found a procession bearing down on him.

At its head were two spearmen as tall as he, ebon-eyed men with capes of leopard skin, the clawed paws hanging across their broad, bare chests. Behind came the drummer, his instrument slung by his side to give free swing to the mallets with which he beat a cadence. A score of men in spiked helms and short, sleeveless mail followed the drummer. Half bore spears and half bows, with quivers on their backs, and all wore wide, white trousers and high, red boots.

Conan's eyes went no further down the cortege than the horsemen who came next, or rather the woman who led them, mounted on a prancing black gelding a hand taller than any her followers rode. Tall she was, and well rounded, a delight both callimastian and callipygean. Her garb of tight tunic and tighter breeches, both of tawny silk, with a scarlet cloak thrown well back across her horse's rump, did naught to hide her curves. Light brown hair, sun-streaked with gold, curled about her shoulders and surrounded a prideful face set with clear gray eyes.

She was a woman worth looking at, Conan thought. And besides, he knew of her, as did every thief in Shadizar. The Lady Jondra was known for many things, her arrogance, her hunting, her racing of horses, but among thieves she was known as the possessor of a necklace and tiara that had set more than one man's mouth watering. Each was set with a flawless ruby, larger than the last joint of a big man's thumb, surrounded by sapphires and black opals. In the Desert men taunted each other with the stealing of them, for of all those who had tried, the only one not taken by the spears of her guards had died with Jondra's own arrows in his eyes. It was said she had been more furious that the thief entered her chambers while she was bathing than at his bungled attempt at theft.

Conan prepared to step from the procession's path,

when the spearmen, not five paces from him now, dropped their spears to the ready. They did not slow their pace, but came on as if the threat should send him scurrying for cover.

The big Cimmerian's face tightened. Did they think him a dog, then, to beat from their way? A young man's pride, dented as much as he could stand in recent days, hardened. He straightened, and his hand went to the worn, leather-wrapped hilt of his broadsword. Dead silence fell among the crowd lining the sides of the street.

The spearmen's eyes widened at the sight of the young giant standing his ground. The streets always cleared before their mistress, the drum usually sufficing, and never more than the gleam of a spearpoint in the sunlight required at most. It came to each in the same instant that this was no apprentice to be chivvied aside. As one man they stopped and dropped into a crouch with spears presented.

The drummer, marching obliviously, continued his pounding until he was between the two spearmen. There his mallets froze, one raised and one against the drumhead, and his eyes darted for a way out. The three men made a barricade across the street that perforce brought the rest of Lady Jondra's cortege to a halt, first the mailed hunters, then the horsemen, and so back down the line, till all stood stopped.

The ludicrousness of it struck Conan, and he felt mirth rising despite himself. How did he get himself into these predicaments, he wondered.

"You there!" a husky woman's voice called. "You,

big fellow with the sword!'' Conan looked up to find
the Lady Jondra staring at him over the heads of her
spearmen and archers. ''If you can stop Zurat and
Tamal in their tracks, perhaps you can face a lion as
well. I always need men, and there are few who
deserve the name in Shadizar. I will take you into my
service.'' A tall, hawk-faced man riding next to her
opened his mouth angrily, but she cut him off with a
gesture. ''What say you? You have the shoulders for
a spearman.''

The laughter broke through, and Conan let it roar,
though he was careful not to take his eyes from the
spearmen or his hand from his sword. Jondra's face
slowly froze in amazement. ''I am already in service,''
he managed, ''to myself. But, my lady, I wish you
good day and will no longer block your passage.'' He
made a sweeping bow—not deep enough to lose sight
of the spear points—and strode to the side of the
street.

For an instant there was stunned silence, then the
Lady Jondra was shouting. ''Zurat! Tamal! March
on! Junio! The beat!''

The spearmen straightened, and the drummer stiffly
took up his cadence again. In moments the procession was moving. Jondra rode past stiffly, her eyes
drifting to the big Cimmerian as if she did not realize
what she did. The hawk-faced man rode beside her,
arguing volubly, but she seemed not to hear.

A knot of barefooted street urchins, all color long
faded from their tattered tunics, suddenly appeared
near Conan. Their leader was a girl, though at an age

when her scrawniness could pass for either sex. Half a head taller than her followers, she swaggered to the muscular youth's side and studied the array of hunters. The lion dogs passed, heavy, snarling brutes with spiked collars, pulling hard on the leashes held by their handlers.

"Dog like that could take your leg off," the girl said. "Big man, you get a spear in your belly, and who's going to pay us?"

"You get paid when you've found her, Laeta," Conan replied. The trophies of the hunt were borne by, skins of leopards and lions, great scimitar antelope horns, the skull of a huge wild ox with horns as thick and long as a man's arm, all held aloft for the view of the onlookers.

She cast a scornful glance at him. "Did I not say as much? We found the wench, and I want those two pieces of silver."

Conan grunted. "When I am sure it's her."

This was not the first report of Tamira he had had. One had been a woman more than twice his age, another a potter's apprentice with only one eye. The last of Jondra's procession passed, pack animals and high-wheeled ox-carts, and the throng that had stood aside flowed together behind like water behind a boat.

"Take me to her," Conan said.

Laeta grumbled, but trotted away down the street, her coterie of hard-eyed urchins surrounding her like a bodyguard. Under every ragged tunic, the Cimmerian knew, was a knife, or more than one. The children of the street preferred to run, but when cornered they were as dangerous as a pack of rats.

To Conan's surprise they moved no closer to the Desert, but rather farther away, into a district peopled by craftsmen. The din of brass-smiths' hammers beat at them, then the stench of the dyers' vats. Smoke from kiln fires rose on all sides. Finally the girl stopped and pointed to a stone building where a sign hanging from chains showed the image of a lion, half-heartedly daubed not too long past with fresh carmine.

"In there?" Conan asked suspiciously. Taverns attracted likes, and a thief would not likely be welcome amid potters and dyers.

"In there," Laeta agreed. She chewed her lip, then sighed. "We will wait out here, big man. For the silver."

Conan nodded impatiently and pushed open the tavern door.

Inside, the Red Lion was arranged differently from the usual tavern. At some time in the past a fire had gutted the building. The ground floor, which had collapsed into the cellar, had never been replaced. Instead, a balcony had been built running around the inside of the building at street level, and the common room was now in what had been the cellar. Even when the sun was high on the hottest day, the common room of the Red Lion remained cool.

From a place by the balcony rail just in front of the door, Conan ran his gaze over the interior of the tavern, searching for a slender female form. A few men stood on the balcony, some lounging against the railing with tankard in hand, most bargaining quietly with doxies for time in the rooms abovestairs. A steady stream of serving girls trotted up and down stairs at the rear of the common room with trays of food and drink, for the kitchen was still on the ground level. Tables scattered across the stone floor below held potters whose arms were flecked with dried clay and leather-aproned metal workers and apprentices with tunics stained by rainbow splashes.

The ever-present trulls, their wisps of silk covering no more here than they did in the Desert, strolled the floor, but as he had expected Conan could see no other women among the tables. Satisfied that Laeta was mistaken or lying, he started to turn for the door. From the corner of his eye he saw a burly potter, with a round-breasted doxy running her fingers through his hair, look away from her bounty to glance curiously at a spot below where the big Cimmerian stood. Another man, his leather apron lying across the table before him and a squealing jade on his knees, paused in his pawing of her to do the same. And yet another man.

Conan leaned to look over the railing, and there Tamira sat beneath him, demurely clothed in pale blue robes, face scrubbed to virginal freshness . . . and a wooden mug upended at her mouth. With a sigh she set the mug on the table upside-down, a signal to the serving girls that she wanted it refilled.

Smiling, Conan slipped the flat throwing knife from his belt. A flicker of his hand, and the black blade quivered in the upturned bottom of her mug. Tamira started, then was still except for the fingers of her left hand drumming on the tabletop. The Cimmerian's smile faded. With a muttered oath he stalked to the stairs and down.

When he reached the table the throwing knife had disappeared. He ignored the wide-eyed looks of men at nearby tables and sat across from her.

"You cost me eight pieces of gold," were his first words.

The corners of Tamira's mouth twitched upward. "So little? I received forty from the Lady Zayella."

Conan's hand gripped the edge of the table till the wood creaked in protest. Forty! "Zarath the Kothian would give a hundred," he muttered, then went on quickly before she could ask why he was then only to receive eight. "I want a word with you, wench."

"And I with you," she said. "I didn't come to a place like this, and let you find me, just to—"

"Let me find you!" he roared. A man at a nearby table hurriedly got up and moved away.

"Of course, I did." Her face and voice were calm, but her fingers began to tap on the table again. "How could I fail to know that every beggar in Shadizar, and a fair number of the trulls, were asking after my whereabouts?"

"Did you think I would forget you?" he asked sarcastically.

She went on as if he had not spoken. "Well, I will not have it. You'll get in my—my uncles' attention.

They'll not take kindly to a stranger seeking after me. I led you here, well away from the Desert, in the hopes they'll not hear of our meeting. You'll find yourself with a blade in your throat, Cimmerian. And for some reason I don't quite understand, I would not like that."

Conan looked at her silently, until under his gaze her large, dark eyes began blinking nervously. Her finger-drumming quickened. "So you do know my country of birth."

"You fool, I am trying to save your life."

"Your uncles look after you?" he said abruptly. "Watch over you? Protect you?"

"You will find out how carefully if you do not leave me alone. And what's that smug grin for?"

"It's just that now I know I'll be your first man." His tone was complacent, but his every muscle tensed.

Tamira's mouth worked in silent incredulity, and scarlet suffused her cheeks. Suddenly a shriek burst from her lips, and the throwing knife was in her hand. Conan threw himself from his bench as her arm whipped forward. Beyond him an appentice yelped and stared disbelieving at the tip of his nose, from which a steady drip of red fell to put new blotches on his dye-stained tunic.

Warily Conan got to his feet. Tamira shook her small fists at him in incoherent fury. At least, he thought, she did not have another of those knives. It would be out, otherwise. "But you must ask me," he said as if there had been no interruption. "That will make up for the eight gold pieces you stole from me, when you ask me.''

"Erlik take you!" she gasped. "Mitra blast your soul! To think I worried . . . to think I. . . . You're nothing but an oaf after all! I hope my uncles do catch you! I hope the City Guard puts your head on a pike! I hope—I hope—oh!" From head to toe she shook with rage.

"I eagerly await our first kiss," Conan said, and dodged her mug, aimed at his head.

Calmly turning his back on her wordless shouts, he strolled up the stairs and out of the tavern. As soon as the door closed behind him, his casual manner disappeared. Urgently he looked for Laeta, and smiled when she appeared with her palm out.

Before she could ask he tossed her two silver coins. "There's more," he said. "I want to know everywhere she goes, and everyone she sees. A silver piece every tenday for you, and the same for your followers." Baratses' gold was disappearing fast, he thought, but with luck it should last just long enough.

Laeta, with her mouth open to bargain, could only nod wordlessly.

Conan smiled in satisfaction. He had Tamira now. After his performance she thought he was a buffoon intent on seduction to salve his pride. He doubted if she even remembered her slip of the tongue. Almost she had said he would get in her way. She planned a theft, and wanted no encumbrance. But this time *he* would get there first, and *she* would find the empty pedestal.

Chapter 4

Much of the Zamoran nobility, the Lady Jondra thought as she strolled through her palace garden, deplored that the last of the Perashanids was a woman. Carefully drawing back the vermilion silk sleeve of her robe, she dabbled her fingers in the sparkling waters of a fountain rimmed with gray-veined marble. From the corner of her eye she watched the man who stood next to her. His handsome, dark-eyed face radiated self-assurance. A heavy gold chain, each link worked with the seal of his family, hung across the crisp pleats of his citrine tunic. Lord Amaranides did not deplore her femininity at all. It meant that all the wealth of the Perashanids went with her hand. If he could manage to secure that hand.

"Let us walk on, Ama," she said, and smiled at his attempt to hide a grimace for the pet name she had given him. He would think the smile was for him, she knew. It was not in him to imagine otherwise.

"The garden is lovely," he said. "But not so lovely as you."

Instead of taking his proffered arm she moved ahead down the slate-tiled walk, forcing him to hurry to catch up to her.

Eventually she would have to wed. The thought brought a sigh of regret, but duty would do what legions of suitors had been unable to. She could not allow the Perashanid line to end with her. Another sigh passed her full lips.

"Why so melancholy, my sweetling?" Amaranides murmured in her ear. "Let me but taste your honey kiss, and I will sweep your moodiness away."

Deftly she avoided his lips, but made no further discouraging move. Unlike most nobly born Zamoran women, she allowed few men so much as a kiss, and none more. But even if she could not bring herself to stop her occasional tweaking of his well-stuffed pomposity, Amaranides must not be put off entirely.

At least he was tall enough, she thought. She never allowed herself to contemplate the reason why she was taller than most Zamoran men, but she had long since decided that her husband must be taller than she. Amaranides was a head taller, but his build was slender. With an idle corner of her mind she sketched the man she wanted. Of noble lineage, certainly. An excellent horseman, archer and hunter, of course. Physically? Taller than Amaranides by nearly a head. Much broader of shoulders, with a deep, powerful chest. Handsome, but more ruggedly so than her companion. His eyes. . . .

Abruptly she gasped as she recognized the man she had drawn in her mind. She had dressed him as a Zamoran nobleman, but it was the sky-eyed street-ruffian who had disrupted her return from the hunt. Her face flooded with scarlet. Blue eyes! A barbarian! Like smoky gray fires her own eyes blazed. That she could consider allowing such a one to touch her, even without realizing it! Mitra! It was worse done without realizing it!

". . . And on my last hunt," Amaranides was saying, "I killed a truly magnificent leopard. Finer than any you've taken, I fancy. It will be a pleasure for me to teach you the finer points of hunting, my little sweetmeat. I. . . ."

Jondra ground her teeth as he rattled blithely on. Still, he *was* a hunter, not to mention nobly born. If he was a fool—and of that there was little doubt in her mind—then he would be all the more easily managed.

"I know why you've come, Ama," she said.

". . . Claws as big as. . . ." The nobleman's voice trailed off, and he blinked uncertainly. "You know?"

She could not keep impatience from her voice. "You want me for your wife. Is that not it? Come." Briskly she set out through the garden toward the fletcher's mound.

Amaranides hesitated, then ran after her. "You don't know how happy you've made me, sweetling. Sweetling? Jondra? Where are you . . . ah!"

Jondra fended off the arms he tried to throw around her with a recurved bow she had taken from a gilded rack standing on a grassy sward. Calmly she slipped a leather bracer onto her left arm for protection from the bowstring. Another bow, a second bracer, and two quivers, clustered fletchings rising above their black-lacquered sides, hung on the rack.

"You must . . . equal me," she said, gesturing toward a small round target of thickly woven straw hanging at the top of a wide wooden frame, which was three times the height of a man, a hundred paces distant. She had intended to say 'best,' but at the last could not bring herself to it. In truth, she did not believe *any* man could best her, either with a bow or on horseback. "I can marry no man who is not my equal as an archer."

Amaranides eyed the target, then took the second bow with a smug smile. "Why so high? No matter. I wager I'll beat you at it." He laughed then, a shocking bray at odds with his handsome features. "I've won many a purse with a bow, but you will be my finest prize."

Jondra's mouth tightened. Shaking back the hanging sleeves of her robes, she nocked an arrow and called, "Mineus!"

A balding man, in the short white tunic of a servant, came from the bushes near the frame and tugged at a rope attached near the target. Immediately the target, no bigger than a man's head, began to slide down a diagonal, and as it slid it swung from side to side on a long wooden arm. Clearly it would take a zig-zag path, at increasing speed, all the way to the ground.

Jondra did not raise her bow until the target had

traversed half the first diagonal. Then, in one motion, she raised, drew and released. With a solid thwack her shaft struck, not slowing the target's descent. Before that arrow had gone home her second was loosed, and a third followed on its heels. As the straw target struck the ground, she lowered her bow with an arrow nocked but unreleased. It was her seventh. Six feathered shafts decorated the target. "The robes hamper me somewhat," she said ruefully. "With your tunic, you may well get more than my six. Let me clothe myself in hunting garb—are you ill, Ama?"

Amaranides' bow hung from a limp hand. He stared, pale of face, at the target. As he turned to her, high color replaced the pallor of his cheeks. His mouth twisted around his words. "I have heard that you delight in besting men, but I had not thought you would claim yourself ready to wed just to lure me to . . . this!" He spat the last word, hurling the bow at the riddled target. "What Brythunian witch-work did you use to magic your arrows?"

Her hands shook with rage as she raised her bow and drew the nocked arrow back to her cheek, but she forced them to be steady. "Remove yourself!" she said grimly.

Mouth falling open, the dark-faced nobleman stared at the arrow pointed at his face. Abruptly he spun about and ran, dodging from side to side, shoulders hunched, as if simultaneously attempting to avoid her arrow and steel himself against its strike.

She followed every skip and leap, keeping the

arrow centered on him until he had disappeared among the shrubs. Then she released the breath in her tight lungs and the tension on her bowstring together. Thoughts she had disciplined from her mind came flooding back.

Lord Karentides, her father, had been a general of the Zamoran Army, as well as the last scion of an ancient house. Campaigning on the Brythunian border he chose a woman from among the prisoners, Camardica, tall and gray-eyed, who claimed to be a priestess. In the normal course of events there would have been nothing strange in this, for Zamoran soldiers often enjoyed themselves with captive Brythunian women, and the Brythunian slaves in Zamora were beyond counting. But Karentides married his captive. Married her and accepted the ostracism that became his.

Jondra remembered his body—his and . . . that woman's—lying in state after the fever that slew so many in the city, sparing neither noble nor beggar. She had been raised, educated, protected as what she was, heiress to vast wealth, to blood of ancient nobility. The marks were on her, though— the height and the accursed eyes of gray—and she had heard the whispers. Half-breed. Savage. Brythunian. She had heard them until her skill with a bow, her ready temper and her disregard of consequences silenced even whispers in her hearing. She was the Lady Jondra of the House Perashanid, daughter of General Lord Karentides, last of a lineage to rival that of King Tiridates himself, and ware to anyone who mentioned aught else.

"He would not have hit it once, my lady," a quiet voice said at her elbow.

Jondra glanced at the balding servant, at the concern on his wrinkled face. "It is not your place to speak so, Mineus," she said, but there was no rebuke in her voice.

Mineus' expression folded into deference. "As you say, my lady. If my lady pleases, the girl sent by the Lady Roxana is here. I put her in the second waiting room, but I can send her away if that is still your wish."

"If I am not to wed," she said, replacing her bow carefully on the rack, "I shall have need of her after all."

The second waiting room was floored with a mosaic of arabesques in green and gold, in the middle of which stood a short, slender girl in a short tunic of dark blue, the color Lady Roxana put on her serving maids. Her dark hair was worked in a simple plait that fell to the small of her back. She kept her eyes on the tiles beneath her small feet as Jondra entered the room.

An ebony table inlaid with ivory held two wax tablets fastened face-to-face with silken cords. Jondra examined the seals on the cords carefully. Few outside the nobility or the merchant classes could write, but servants had been known to try altering their recommendations. There were no signs of tampering here. She cut the cords and read.

"Why do you wish to leave the Lady Roxana's service?" she asked abruptly. "Lyana? That's your name?"

"Yes, my lady," the girl answered without raising her head. "I want to become a lady's maid, my lady. I worked in the Lady Roxana's kitchens, but her handmaidens trained me. The Lady Roxana had no place for another handmaiden, but she said that you sought one."

Jondra frowned. Did the chit not even have enough spirit to meet her eyes? She abhorred a lack of spirit, whether in dogs or horses or servants. "I need a girl to tend my needs on the hunt. The last two found the rigors too great. Do you think your desire to be a lady's maid will survive heat and flies and sand?"

"Oh, yes, my lady."

Slowly Jondra walked around the girl studying her from every angle. She certainly *looked* sturdy enough to withstand a hunting camp. With fingertips she raised the girl's chin. "Lovely," she said, and thought she saw a spark in those large, dark eyes. Perhaps there was some spirit here after all. "I'll not have my hunts disrupted by spearmen panting after a pretty face, girl. See you cast no eyes at my hunters." Jondra smiled. There had definitely been a flash of anger that time.

"I am a maiden, my lady," the girl said with the faintest trace of tightness in her voice.

"Of course," Jondra said noncommittally. Few serving girls were, though all seemed to think the condition made them more acceptable to their mistresses. "I'm surprised the Lady Roxana allowed you to leave her, considering the praises she heaps on your head." She tapped the wax tablet with a fingernail. "In time I will discover if you deserve them. In any case, know that I will allow no hint of disobedience, lying, stealing or laziness. I do not beat my servants as often as some, but trangression in these areas will earn you stripes." She watched the sparks in the girl's eyes replaced with eagerness as the meaning of her words broke through.

"My lady, I swear that I will serve you as such a great lady deserves to be served."

Jondra nodded. "Mineus, show her to the servants' quarters. And summon Arvaneus."

"It shall be done, my lady."

She dismissed the matter from her mind then, the sounds of Mineus leading the girl from the room seeming to fade to insignificance. Replacing the tablets on the ebony table, she crossed the room to a tall, narrow cabinet of profusely carved rosewood. The doors opened to reveal shelves piled with scrolls of parchment, each bound with a ribbon. Hastily she pawed through the pale cylinders.

The incident with Amaranides had crystallized a decision. That the whispers about her parentage were still being bruited about was reason enough to end her consideration of marriage. Instead. . . .

Amaranides had said she liked to best men. Could she help it that men, with their foolish pride, could not accept the fact that she was better than they, whether with bow or horse or on the hunt? Well, now she would best them properly. She would do what none of them had either the skill or the courage to do.

She untied the ribbon about a scroll and searched down the parchment until she found what she sought.

> The beast, my lady, is said to be scaled like a serpent, but to move on legs. Winnowing out obvious exaggerations caused by fear, I can reliably report that it has slain and eaten both men and cattle. Its habitat, my lady, seems, however, to be the Kezankian Mountains near the border between Zamora and Brythunia. With the current unrest of the hill tribes, I cannot suggest. . . .

The parchment crumpled in her hands. She would bring this strange beast's hide back as her trophy. Let one of Amaranidcs' ilk suggcst he could do as much. Let him just dare.

Tamira scurried down palace corridors in Mineus' wake, barely hearing when the balding old man told her of her duties, or when he spoke to other servants. Until the very last moment she had not been certain her plan would work, even after so much planning and labor.

Forty gold pieces she had obtained from Zayella, and all had gone in preparation for this. Most went to Roxana's chamberlain, who provided the use of the Lady's private seal. There would be no checking, though, to trip her up, for the Lady Roxana had departed the city a day past. Tamira allowed herself a smile. In a day or two she would have Jondra's fabulous necklace and tiara.

"Give attention, girl," Mineus said impatiently. "You must know this to help prepare for the Lady Jondra's hunt."

Tamira blinked. "Hunt? But she just returned from a hunt."

"You saw me speak to Arvaneus, the chief huntsman. No doubt you will depart as soon as supplies are gathered."

Panic flashed through her. It had been none of her intention to actually go on one Jondra's forays. There was no point to her sweating in a tent while the jewels remained in Shadizar. Of course, they would be there when she returned. But so might the Lady Roxana. "I—I have to see . . . about my belongings," she stammered. "I left clothing at the Lady Roxana's palace. And my favorite pin. I must fetch—"

Mineus cut her short. "When you've had instructions as to your duties in preparing for the hunt. Not only must you see that my lady's clothing and jewels are packed, but you must see to her perfumes, the soaps and oils for her bathing, and—"

"She—my lady takes her jewels hunting?"

"Yes, girl. Now pay attention. My lady's rouges and powders—"

"You mean a few bracelets and brooches," Tamira insisted.

The old man rubbed his bald spot and sighed. "I mean nothing of the sort, girl. Of an evening my lady often adorns herself to dine in her finest. Now, since you seem distracted for some reason, I will see you through your tasks.''

For the rest of the morning and into the afternoon Tamira was prodded and pushed from one labor to the next, always under Mineus' watchful eye. She folded Jondra's garments of silks and laces—three times she folded them before reaching Mineus' satisfaction—and packed them in wicker panniers. Rare perfumes from Vendhya and powders from far Khitai, rouges from Sultanapur, costly oils and unguents from the corners of the world, all she wrapped in soft cloths and packed, with the balding old man hovering close to remind her that every vial and jar must be handled as gently as a swaddling child. Then, staggering under the weighty panniers, she and another serving-woman carried them down to the stableyard, where the pack-animals would be loaded on the morrow.

On each trip through Jondra's chambers, the chests for transporting the noblewoman's jewelry, thick-sided boxes of iron, made her mouth water. They sat so tantalizingly against a tapestry-hung wall. But they were empty iron now, for they would not be filled until the last instant. Still, the gems would be going with her. She could not help smiling.

Aching from the unaccustomed labor, Tamira found that Mineus had led her to a side door of the palace. ''Fetch your belongings, girl,'' he said, ''and return quickly. There will be more work.''

Before she could speak she had been thrust outside, and the door closed in her face. For a long moment she stared wonderingly at the red-painted wood. She had forgotten her panic-induced invention of possessions. Her original plan called for remaining inside Jondra's palace until the necklace and tiara were in her hands. In that way Conan would never discover what she was up to. The huge barbarian seemed intent on. . . .

It dawned on her that she *was* outside the palace, and she spun around to study the narrow street. A turbanned Kezankain hillman squatted disconsolately against a wall across the street, and a few ragged urchins played tag on the rough paving stones. She heaved a sigh of relief. There was neither a beggar nor a doxy in sight. Her uncles could provide a bundle to satisfy Mineus. Keeping a careful watch for Conan's many eyes, she hurried down the street.

Unseen by her, three of the urchins broke off their play and trailed after her.

The hillman watched her go with lustful eyes, then reluctantly returned to his surveillance of the palace.

Chapter 5

At a corner table in Abuletes' common room, Conan glowered into a leathern jack half-filled with cheap Kothian wine. Semiramis, in a girdle of coins and two strips of thin scarlet silk, was seated in the lap of a Turanian coiner across the crowded room, but for once that was not the reason for the Cimmerian's dour face. What remained of Baratses' two gold pieces had been lessened at dice the previous night. With all of his mind on Tamira, he had given no thought to how to get more. And worst, he had had no word from Laeta. It was only a day since he had set the urchin to watch Tamira, but he was certain—as certain as if he had been told by the dark-eyed thief herself—that she moved already on the theft she planned. The theft he had vowed to beat her to. And he had no word!

Grimacing, he raised his wine and gulped the remainder of it down. When he lowered the jack a tall, bony man stood across the table from him. A fine

75

black Khauranian cloak, edged with cloth of gold, was pulled tightly around him as if to hide his identity.

"What do you want, Baratses?" Conan grumbled. "I keep the two gold pieces for the attempt, and you should be thankful to have it made so cheaply."

"Do you have a room in this . . . establishment?" The spice merchant's black eyes darted about the raucous tavern as if he expected to be attacked at any moment. "I would talk with you in privacy."

Conan shook his head in disbelief. The fool had obviously dressed himself in what he considered plain fashion, but just as obviously he was no denizen of the Desert. His passage had certainly been noted, and footpads no doubt awaited nine deep in the street for his departure, but here, where he was safe from such, he feared robbery.

"Come," Conan said, and led the way up the rickety wooden stairs at the back of the common room.

His own room was a simple box of rough wooden planks, with a narrow window shuttered in a vain attempt to keep out the stench of the alley behind the tavern. A wide, low bed, a table with one short leg, and a lone stool were all the furnishings. The Cimmerian's few possessions—aside from the ancient broadsword he always wore—hung on pegs in one wall.

Baratses glanced around the room disdainfully, and Conan bristled. "I cannot afford a palace. Yet. Now, why are you here? Something more to be stolen?

You'll give a fair price this time, or find someone else.''

"You've not yet fulfilled your last commission, Cimmerian.'' Though the door was closed, the merchant kept his cloak clutched about him. "I have the rest of your gold here, but where is my goblet? I know Samarides no longer possesses it.''

"Nor do I," Conan replied ruefully. "Another was there before me.'' He hesitated, but could not rid himself of the belief that the man deserved at least some information for his two gold pieces. "I have heard the Lady Zayella has the goblet now.''

"So she offered you more than I," Baratses murmured. "I had heard you had some odd concept of honor, but I see I was wrong.''

The Cimmerian's eyes grew icy. "Do not call me liar, merchant. Another took the goblet.''

"The room is close,'' Baratses said. "I am hot.'' He twitched the cloak from his shoulders, swirling it before him.

Instinct flared a warning in Conan. As the cloak moved aside his big hand slapped down to grasp Baratses' wrist, stopping a black-bladed Karpashian dagger a handspan from his middle. "Fool!'' he said.

Blood and teeth sprayed from the merchant's face beneath Conan's fist. The dagger dropped from nerveless fingers and struck the floor no more than an instant before Baratses himself.

The big Cimmerian frowned at the man lying unconscious before him. A sheath on Baratses' forearm had held the black blade. Conan bent to remove that, and tossed it and the dagger atop the cloak. "An attempt on my life," he muttered finally, "surely earns me the gold you brought."

Unfastening the merchant's purse from his belt, Conan emptied it onto his palm. There was no gold, only silver and copper. He counted it and grimaced. Three coppers more than a single gold piece. It seemed his death had been intended whether he had the goblet or not. Pouring the coins back into the purse, he added it to the dagger and sheath.

On the floor Baratses stirred and moaned.

Knotting his fist in the bony man's tunic, Conan lifted him erect and shook him till his eyes fluttered open. Baratses let out a gurgling groan as his tongue explored splintered teeth.

"I do not have the goblet," the Cimmerian said grimly. Easily he hoisted the merchant's feet clear of the floor. "I have never had the goblet." He took a step and smashed Baratses against the shutter, which burst open. The bloody-faced man dangled above the alley at arm's length from the window. "And if I ever see you again, I'll break the rest of your teeth." Conan opened his hand.

Baratses' wail cut off as he landed with a squelch in equal parts of mud, offal and the emptyings of chamber pots. A scrawny dog, disturbed at its rootings, began to bark at him furiously. Scrambling shakily to his feet, Baratses stared wildly about him, then broke into a slipping, sliding run. "Murder!" he screamed. "Murder!"

Conan sighed as he watched the merchant disappear down the alley. His cries would bring no aid in the Desert, but once he was beyond those cramped streets the City Guard would come quickly enough. And listen attentively to a respectable merchant's tale. Perhaps it would have been better had he slit the man's throat, yet murder had never been his way. He would have to leave the city for a time, until the furor died down. The fist that had broken Baratses' teeth pounded the window frame. And by the time he returned Tamira would have accomplished her theft. He might never even know what it was, much less in time to get there first.

Hastily he made his preparations. The contents of Baratses' purse were added to his own. The dagger in its sheath he fastened to his left forearm, then settled the black cloak about his broad shoulders. It fit a trifle snugly, but was ten times better than what he had.

He frowned at a lump over his chest, and felt inside the cloak. A small pouch of cloth was sewn there. From it he drew a small silver box, its lid set with blue gems. Inferior sapphires, his experienced eye told him. He flipped it open; his lip curled contemptuously at the sickly verduous powder within. Pollen from the green lotus of Vendhya. It seemed Baratses liked his dreams to come when he desired them. The small quantity in his hand would bring ten gold pieces. Upending the silver box, he tapped it against the heel of his hand to make sure all of the pollen fell to the floor. He did not deal in such things.

Quickly he ran an eye over the rest of his possessions. There was nothing there worth the bother of bundling. Near two years of thievery, and this was all he had to show for it. A fool like Baratses could throw away on stolen dreams as much as he could earn in a night of risking his life. Pushing open the door, he slapped the worn leather hilt of his broadsword with a mirthless laugh. "This is all I need anyway," he told himself.

At the bar Abuletes came slowly in response to the big Cimmerian's beckoning gesture. "I need a horse," Conan said when the fat innkeeper was finally before him. "A good horse. Not one ready for the boneyard."

Abuletes' black eyes, deepset in wells of suet, went from the cloak on Conan's shoulders to the stairs. "You need to leave Shadizar quickly, Cimmerian?"

"There's no body to be found," Conan reassured him. "Just a disagreement with a man who can get the ear of the City Guard."

"Too bad," Abuletes grunted. " 'Tis cheaper to dispose of a body than to purchase a horse. But I know a man—" Suddenly he glared past Conan's shoulder. "You! Out! I'll have none of you filthy little thieves in my place!"

Conan glanced over his shoulder. Laeta stood just inside the door, glaring fiercely back at the tavern-keeper. "She has come to see me," the Cimmerian said.

"She?" Abuletes said incredulously, but he was speaking to Conan's back.

"You have news of Tamira?" Conan asked when he reached the girl. It was like his luck of late, he thought, that the news would come when he could not use it.

Laeta nodded, but did not speak. Conan dug two silver pieces from his purse, but when she stretched out a hand for them he lifted them out of her reach and looked at her questioningly.

"All right, big man," she sighed. "But I had better get my coin. Yestermorn your wench went to the palace of the Lady Jondra."

"Jondra!" So she was after the necklace and tiara. And he had to leave the city. Grinding his teeth, he tossed the coins to Laeta. "Why didn't you tell me then?"

She tucked the silver under her torn tunic. "Because she left again. And," she added reluctantly, "we lost her trail in the Katara Bazaar. But this morning I set Urias to watch Jondra's palace, and he saw her again. This time she left dressed like a serving girl and riding a supply cart in Jondra's hunting party. The lot of them departed the city by the Lion Gate. A good six turns of the glass ago, it was. Urias took his time telling me, and I'm docking him his share of this silver for it."

Conan studied the girl, wondering if she had spun this tale. It seemed too fantastic. Unless . . . unless Tamira had discovered Jondra was taking the fabled necklace and tiara with her. But on a hunt? No matter. He had to leave Shadizar anyway. As well ride north and see for himself what Tamira was up to.

He started to turn away, then stopped, looking at Laeta's dirt-smudged face and big, wary eyes, truly seeing her for the first time. "Wait here," he told her. She eyed him quizzically, but stood there as he walked away.

He found Semiramis leaning against the wall at the back of the common room, one foot laid across her knee so she could rub it. Quickly he separated out half the coin in his purse and pressed it into her hand.

"Conan," she protested, "you know I'll not take money from—"

"It's for her," he said, jerking his head toward Laeta, who was watching him suspiciously. Semiramis arched a questioning eyebrow. "In another year she'll not be able to pass as a boy any longer," he explained. "Already she's putting dirt on her face to hide how pretty she is. I thought, maybe, that you. . . ." He shrugged awkwardly, unsure of what he did mean.

Semiramis raised herself on tiptoes and brushed her lips against his cheek.

"That's no kiss," he laughed. "If you want to say goodbye—"

She laid her fingers against his lips. "You are a better man than you try to pretend, Cimmerian." With that she slipped by him.

Wondering if women were made by the same gods

as men, he watched her approach Laeta. The two spoke quietly, looked at him, then moved toward an empty table together. As they sat, he suddenly recalled his own needs. He strode back to the bar and caught the tavernkeeper's arm as the fat man passed.

"About this horse, Abuletes. . . ."

Chapter 6

Dark hung silently over Shadizar, at least in the quarter where lay the Perashanid palace. A hatchet-faced man in a filthy turban and stained leather jerkin, his beard divided into three braids, moved from the shadows, freezing when the barking of a dog rent the night. Then quiet came again.

"Farouz," the bearded man called softly. "Jhal. Tirjas."

The three men named appeared from the dark, each followed by half a score other turbanned Kezankian hillmen.

"The true gods guide our blades, Djinar," one man murmured as he passed hatchet-face.

Booted feet thudding on the paving stones, each small column hurried toward its appointed goal. Farouz would take his men over the garden's west wall, Jhal over the north. Tirjas was to watch the front of the palace and assure that no one left . . . alive.

"Come," Djinar commanded, and ten grim hillmen hurried after him to the east wall of the palace garden.

At the base of the wall two of his men bent to present cupped hands for his booted feet. Boosted thus, Djinar caught the top of the wall and scrambled over to drop inside. Moonlight put a silver glow on the trees and flowers of the garden. He wondered briefly at the labor involved. So much sweat, and for plants. Truly the men of the cities were mad.

Soft thuds announced the arrival of his companions. Swords were drawn with the susurration of steel on leather, and from one man came a fierce mutter. "Death to the unbelievers!"

Djinar hissed for silence, unwilling to speak lest his feelings at being within a city became plain in his voice. So many people gathered in one place. So many buildings. So many walls, closing him in. He motioned the hillmen to follow.

Silently the stony-eyed column slipped through the garden. No doors barred their entrance to the palace. It was going well, Djinar thought. The others would be entering the palace at other places. No alarm had been given. The blessings of the old gods must be on them, as Basrakan Imalla had said.

Abruptly a man in the white tunic of a servant appeared before him, mouth opening to shout. Djinar's tulwar moved before he could think, the tip of the curved blade slicing open the other man's throat.

As the corpse twitched in a pool of crimson, spreading across the marble floor, Djinar found his nervousness gone. "Spread out," he commanded. "None must live to give an alarm. Go!"

Growling deep in their throats, his men scattered with ready blades. Djinar ran as well, seeking the chamber that had been described to him by a sweating Akkadan beneath the iron gaze of Basrakan Imalla. Three more servants, roused by pounding boots, fell beneath his bloody steel. All were unarmed, one was a woman, but all were unbelievers, and he gave them no chance to cry out.

Then he was at his goal, and it was as the plump man had said. Large square tiles of red, black and gold covered the floor in geometric patterns. The walls were red and black brick to the height of a man's waist. Furnishings he did not notice. That lamps were lit so that he could see them was all that was important.

Still gripping his sanguine sword, Djinar hurried to the nearest corner and pushed against a black brick four down from the top row and four out from the corner. He gave a satisfied grunt when it sank beneath his pressure. Quickly he moved to the other three corners in turn; three more black bricks sank into the wall.

A clatter of boots in the corridor brought him to his feet, tulwar raised. Farouz and other hillmen burst into the room.

"We must hurry," Farouz snarled. "A bald-headed old man broke Karim's skull with a vase and escaped into the garden. We'll never find him before he raises an alarm."

Djinar bit back an oath. Hurriedly he positioned four men on their knees, forming the corners of a square beside widely separated golden tiles. "Press all together," he ordered. "Together, mind you. Now!"

With sharp clicks the four tiles were depressed as one. A grinding noise rose from beneath their feet. Slowly, two thick sections of the floor swung up to reveal stairs leading down.

Djinar darted down those stairs, and found himself in a small chamber carved from the stone beneath the palace. Dim light filtered from above, revealing casket-laden shelves lining the walls. In haste he opened a casket, then another. Emeralds and sapphires on golden chains. Opals and pearls mounted in silver brooches. Carved ivories and amber. But not what he sought. Careless of the treasures he handled, the hillman spilled the contents of caskets on the floor. Gems and precious metals poured to the marble. His feet kicked wealth enough for a king, but he gave it not a second glance. With a curse he threw aside the last empty casket and ran back up the stairs.

More hillmen had come, crowding the room. Now some pushed past him to the chamber below. Squabbling, they stuffed their tunics with gems and gold.

"The Eyes of Fire are not here," Djinar announced. The men below, panting with greed, paid no mind, but those in the chamber with him grew long faces.

"Perhaps the woman took them with her," suggested a man with a scar where his left ear had been.

Farouz spat loudly. "It was you, Djinar, who said

wait. The strumpet goes to hunt, you said. She will take her guards, and we shall have an easier time of it.''

Djinar's thin lips curled back from his teeth. ''And you, Farouz,'' he snarled. ''Did you cry for us to press on? Did you spend no time in the places where women barter their flesh for coin?'' He clamped his teeth on his rage. The feeling of walls trapping him returned. What was to be done? To return to Basrakan Imalla empty-handed after being commanded to bring the Eyes of Fire. . . . He shuddered at the thought. If the Zamoran jade had the Eyes of Fire, then she must be found. ''Does none of these vermin still live?''

Mutters of negation filled the room, but Farouz said, ''Jhal keeps a wench alive till his pleasure is spent. Do you now abandon the Imalla's quest to join him?''

Djinar's dagger was suddenly in his hand. He tested the edge on a well-calloused thumb. ''I go to ask questions,'' he said, and strode from the room.

Behind him the hubbub of argument over the looting rose higher.

Chapter 7

Conan let his reins fall on the neck of his horse, moving at a slow walk, and took a long pull on his water-skin. His expression did not change at the stale taste of the tepid fluid. He had drunk worse at times when the sun did not beat down so strongly from a cloudless sky as it did now, though it had risen not three handspans above the horizon. His cloak was rolled and bound behind his saddle pad, and a piece of his tunic was held on his head like a kaffiyeh by a leather cord. Rolling hills, with here and there an outcrop of rock or a huge, half-buried boulder, stretched as far as the eye could discern, with never a tree, nor any growth save sparse patches of rough grass.

Twice since leaving Shadizar he had crossed the tracks of very large bodies of men, and once he had seen Zamoran infantry in the distance, marching north. He kept himself from their sight. It did not seem likely that Baratses had influence enough to set the army on his trail, but a man in Conan's profession quickly learned to avoid chance encounters with large numbers of soldiers. Life was more peaceful, less complicated without soldiers. Of the Lady Jondra's hunting party he had seen no sign.

Plugging the spout of the skin, he slung it from his shoulder and returned to a study of the tracks he followed now. A single horse, lightly laden. Perhaps a woman rider.

He booted the roan into a trot, its quickest pace. He intended to have a word with Abuletes when he returned to Shadizar, a quiet converse about messages sent to horse traders. The tavernkeeper's friend had denied having another animal beside this gelding on its last legs, and bargained as if he knew the big youth had reason to leave Shadizar quickly. Conan dug in his heels again, but the animal would move no faster.

Snarls, growing louder as he rode, drifted to him over the next rise. Topping the swell of ground, he took in the scene below in one glance. Half a score of wolves quarreled over the carcass of a horse. Some eyed him warily without ceasing their feast. Twenty paces away the Lady Jondra crouched precariously atop a boulder, her bow clutched in one hand. Five more of the massive gray beasts waited below, their eyes intent on her.

Suddenly one of them took a quick step forward and leaped for the girl on the rock. Desperately she drew her feet up and swung the bow like a club. The wolf twisted in mid-air; powerful jaws closed on the bow, ripping it from her grasp. The force of it pulled her forward, slipping down the side of the boulder. She gave a half-scream, grabbed frantically at the stone, and hung there, closer now to the creatures below. She pulled her legs up, but the next leaper would reach them easily.

"Crom," Conan muttered. There was no time for planning, or even for conscious decisions. His heels thudded into the roan's ribs, goading it into a sliding charge down the hillside. "Crom!" he bellowed, and his broadsword whispered from its worn shagreen scabbard.

The wolfpack gained its feet as one, gray forms crouching to await him. Jondra stared at him in wild disbelief. The roan, eyes wide and whinnying in terror, suddenly broke into a gallop. Two of the wolves darted for the horse's head, and two more dashed in behind to snap at its hamstrings. A fore-hoof shattered a broad gray-furred head. Conan's blade whistled down to split the skull of a second wolf. The roan kicked back with both hind legs, splintering the ribs of a third, but the fourth sank gleaming fangs deep into one of those legs. Screaming, the horse stumbled and fell.

Conan stepped from his saddle pad as the animal went down, just in time to meet leaping gray death with a slashing blade. Half cut in two the great wolf dropped. Behind him Conan heard the roan scramble to its feet, whinnying frantically, and the solid thuds of hooves striking home. There was no opportunity to so much as glance at his mount, though, or even to look at Jondra, for the rest of the pack swarmed around him.

Desperately the big Cimmerian cut and hacked at deadly shapes that darted and slashed like gray demons. Blood splashed cinereous fur, and not all of it was theirs, for their teeth were like razors, and he could not keep them all from him. With cold certainty he knew he could not afford to go down, even for an instant. Let him once get off his feet, and he was meat for the eating. Somehow he managed to get the Karpashian dagger into his left hand, and laid about him with two blades. All thought left him save battle; he fought with as pure a fury as the wolves themselves, asking no quarter and giving none. To fight was all he knew. To fight, and let the losers go to the ravens.

As suddenly as the combat had begun it was ended. One instant steel battled slashing fangs, the next massive gray forms were loping away over the hills, one limping on three legs. Conan looked around him, half wondering that he still lived. Nine wolves lay as heaps of blood-soaked fur. The roan was down again, and this time it would not rise again. A gaping wound in its throat dripped blood into a dark pool that was already soaking into the rocky soil.

A scrabbling sound drew Conan's eyes. Jondra slid from the boulder and took her bow from the ground. Snug tunic and riding breeches of russet silk delineated every curve of her full-breasted form. Lips pursed, she examined the gouges in the bow's glued layers of bone and wood. Her hands shook.

"Why did you not put arrows into a few?" Conan demanded. "You might have saved yourself before I came."

"My quiver. . . ." Her voice trailed off at the sight of her half-eaten horse, but she visibly steeled herself and went to the carcass. From under the bloody mass she tugged a quiver. A crack ran down one side of the black lacquerwork. Checking the arrows, she discarded three that were broken, then slung the quiver on her back. "I had no chance to reach this," she said, adjusting the cords that held the lacquered box on her back. "The first wolf hamstrung my gelding before I even saw it. It was Hannuman's own luck I made it to that rock."

"This is no country for a woman to ride alone," Conan grumbled as he retrieved the rolled cloak and wiped his bloody blade on his saddle pad. He knew he should take a different course with this woman. He had, after all, ridden halfway across Zamora for the express purpose of getting close enough to steal her gems. But there he stood with his horse dead, a dozen gashes that, if not serious still burned and bled, and no mind to walk easily with anyone.

"Guard your tongue!" Jondra snapped. "I've ridden—" Suddenly she seemed to see him fully for the first time. Taking a step back, she raised the bow before her as if it were a shield. "You!" Her voice was a breathless whisper. "What do you do here?"

"What I do is walk, since my horse is slain in the saving of your life. For which, I mind me, I've heard no word of thanks, nor an offer to bind my wounds in your camp.''

Mouth dropping open, Jondra stared at him, astonishment warring with anger on her face. Drawing a deep breath, she shook herself as if waking from a dream. "You saved my life . . ." she began, then trailed off. "I do not even know your name."

"I am called Conan. Conan of Cimmeria."

Jondra made a small bow, and her smile trembled only a little. "Conan of Cimmeria, I offer you my heartfelt thanks for my life. As well, I offer the use of my camp for as long as you choose to stay." She looked at the wolf carcasses and shuddered. "I have taken many trophies," she said unsteadily, "but I never thought to be one. The skins are yours, of course."

The Cimmerian shook his head, though it pained him to abandon useful pelts. And valuable ones, too, could they be gotten back to Shadizar. He hefted his waterskin, showing a long rent made by slashing jaws. A last few drops of water dripped to the ground.

"Without water, we can waste no time with skinning in this heat." He shaded his eyes with a broad palm and measured how far the sun had yet to rise to reach its zenith. "It will get hotter before it cools. How far is it to your camp?"

"On horses we could be there by the time the sun is high, or shortly after. On foot. . . ." She shrugged, making her heavy breasts move under the tight silk of her tunic. "I walk little, and so am no judge."

Conan made an effort to keep his mind on the

matter at hand. "Then we must start now. You will have to keep up, for if we stop in this heat we shall likely never move again. Now, which way?"

Jondra hesitated, clearly as unused to taking commands as to walking. Haughty gray eyes dueled with cool sapphire blue; it was gray that fell. Without another word, but with an irritated expression painted on her features, the tall noblewoman fitted a shaft to her bow and began walking, headed south of the rising sun.

Conan stared after her before following, and not for the pleasant rolling motion of her rump. The fool woman had not wanted him behind her. Did she fear he would take her by force? And why had she seemed shaken by fear when she recognized him? Slowly, however, his questions were submerged in the pleasure of watching her make her way over the rolling hills. The silk riding breeches fit her buttocks like skin, and the view as she toiled upslope ahead of him was enough to make any man forget himself.

The sun climbed on, a ball of luteous fire baking the air dry. Shimmers rose from the rocky ground, and boot soles burned as if they rested on coals. Every breath sucked moisture from the lungs, dried the throat. Across the sky marched the sun, to its zenith and beyond, roasting the flesh, baking the brain.

The sun, Conan realized as he labored uphill in Jondra's wake, had replaced the woman as the center of his thoughts. He tried to calculate the time he had left to find water, the time before the strength of his thews began to fail. The effort of wetting his cracking lips was wasted, for the dampness did not last beyond the doing. He saw no use in offering up prayers. Crom, the Lord of the Mound, the god of his harsh native land, listened to no prayers, accepted no votive offerings. Crom gave a man but two gifts, life and will, and never another. Will would carry him till dark, he decided. Then, having survived a day, he would set about surviving the night, and then the next day, and the next night.

Of the girl he was not so sure. Already she had begun to stagger, tripping over stones she would easily have stepped over when they left the horses. Abruptly a rock smaller than her fist turned under her boot, and she fell heavily. To hands and knees she rose, but no further. Her head hung weakly, and her sides heaved with the effort of drawing a decent breath from the bone-dry air.

Scrambling up beside her, Conan pulled her to her feet. She hung limply from his hands. "Is this the right direction, girl? Is it?"

"How—dare—you," she managed through cracked lips.

Fiercely he shook her; her head lolled on her neck. "The direction, girl! Tell me!"

Unsteadily she looked around them. "Yes," she said finally. "I—think."

With a sigh, Conan lifted her over his shoulder.

"Not—dignified," she panted. "Put—me—down."

"There's no one to see," he told her. And perhaps never would be, he told himself. A well-honed instinct for direction would keep him moving on the path Jondra had set as long as he was able to move; an instinct for survival and an indomitable will would keep him moving long after the limits of ordinary human endurance had been breeched. He would find her camp. If she actually followed the true path. If he had not waited too late to question her. If. . . .

Putting his doubts and Jondra's weak struggles alike from his mind, Conan set out slightly to the south of the line the sun had followed in rising. Constantly his eyes searched for signs of water, but in vain. It was too much to hope for palm fronds waving above a spring. Now, however, he could not find even the plants that would show him where to dig for a seep hole. No trace of green met his eyes save the short, wiry grass that could grow where a lizard would die of thirst. The sun blazed its way westward.

Conan's gaze swept toward the horizon. No smoke marked a campsite, no track disturbed the stony flanks of the hills before him. A steady, ground-eating pace he kept, tirelessly at first, then, as shadows lengthened before him, with an iron determination that denied the possibility of surrender. With water the coming night would have been a haven. Without it, there would be no stopping, for if they stopped they might well never take another step.

Darkness swooped, with no twilight. The stretching shadows seemed to merge and permeate the air in moments. The searing heat dissipated quickly. Stars blinked into being, like flecks of crystal on black velvet, and with them came a chill that struck to the bone as fiercely as had the sun. Jondra stirred on his shoulder and murmured faintly. Conan could not make out what she said, nor waste the energy to wonder what it had been.

He began to stumble, and he knew it was not only the dark. His throat was as dry as the rocks that turned under his feet, and the cold gave little relief to the sun-cracked skin of his face. All he could see were the unwinking stars. Locking his eyes on the horizon, a thin line where sable merged into ebon, he trudged on. Abruptly he realized that three of those stars did seem to shimmer. And they lay below the horizon. Fires.

Forcing his feet to move faster, Conan half-ran toward the camp, for such it must be, whether Jondra's or another. Whoever's camp it was, they must go in, for they had to have water. With his free hand he loosened his sword in its scabbard. They needed water, and he meant to have it.

The 'stars' clearly became fires built high, surrounded by two-wheeled carts and round tents, with picket lines of animals beyond. Conan stumbled into the firelight; men in short mail tunics and baggy white trousers leaped to their feet. Hands reached for spears and tulwars.

The Cimmerian let Jondra fall and put a hand to his sword hilt. ''Water,'' he croaked. The one word was all he could manage.

''What have you done?'' a tall hawk-faced man demanded. Conan worked for the moisture to ask what the man meant, but the other did not wait. "Kill him!" he snarled.

Conan's broadsword slid smoothly free, and it was not the only steel bared to gleam in the light of the fires. Some men raised their spears to throw.

"No!" The faint command came in a thirst-hoarsened voice. "No, I say!"

Conan risked a glance from the corner of his eye. One of the mail-shirted men held a water-skin solicitously to Jondra's lips, and her shoulders were supported by Tamira, in the short, white tunic of a servant.

Not lowering his sword—for few of the others had lowered theirs—Conan began to laugh, a dry, rasping sound of relief. It hurt his throat, but he did not care.

"But, my lady," the hawk-faced man protested. Conan remembered him, now, at Jondra's shoulder that day in Shadizar.

"Be silent, Arvaneus," Jondra barked. She took two more thirsty gulps from the waterskin, then pushed it aside and held out an imperious hand, demanding to be helped to her feet. The man with the waterskin hastened to comply. She stood unsteadily, but pushed him aside when he tried to support her. "This man saved me from wolves, Arvaneus, and carried me when I could not walk. While you huddled by the fires, he saved my life. Give him water. Tend his hurts, and see to his comfort."

Hesitantly, eying Conan's bare blade, the man with the waterskin handed it to the big Cimmerian.

Arvaneus spread his hands in supplication. "We

searched, my lady. When you did not return, we
searched until dark, then built the fires high that you
might see them and be guided to the camp. At first
light we would have—''

"At first light I would have been dead!" Jondra
snapped. "I will retire to my tent now, Arvaneus,
and give thanks to Mitra that my survival was not left
to you. Attend me, Lyana." Her rigid-backed departure was spoiled slightly by a stumble, and she muttered a curse as she ducked into her scarlet-walled
pavillion.

Conan cast an eye about the encampment—the
tulwars and spears were no longer in evidence—and
sheathed his own blade. As he was raising the
waterskin, he met Arvaneus' gaze. The huntsman's
black eyes were filled with a hatred rooted in his
marrow. And he was not the only one staring at the
Cimmerian. Tamira's glare was one of frustration.

"Lyana!" Jondra called from her tent. "Attend
me, girl, or. . . ." The threat was implicit in her
tone.

For the barest moment Tamira hesitated, giving
Conan a well-honed look, then she darted for the
tent.

Arvaneus' face was still a mask of malignity, but
Conan neither knew the reason nor cared. All that
mattered was that he would now surely reach the
necklace and tiara before the young woman thief.
That and nothing more. With a rasping chuckle he
tilted up the waterskin and drank deeply.

Chapter 8

The tall, gray-eyed young man kicked his horse into a trot as the lay of the country told him he neared his village. The last wisps of morning fog lingered among the towering forest oaks, as it often did in this part of Brythunia, not far from the Kezankian Mountains. Then the village itself came in view. A few low, thatch-roofed houses of stone, those of the village's wealthiest men, were dotted among the wattle structures that clustered around two dirt streets that lay at right angles to each other.

People crowded the street as he rode into the village. "Eldran!" they shouted, and dogs ran beside his horse, adding their barking to the uproar. "You have come! Boudanecea said you would!" The men were dressed as he, their tunics embroidered at the neck, with cross-gaitered fur leggings that rose to the knee. The women's dresses were longer versions of the tunics, but in a profusion of scarlets and yellows and blues where the men's were brown and gray, and embroidered at hem and at the ends of the sleeves as well.

"Of course I've come," he said as he dismounted. "Why should I not?" They gathered about him, each trying to get close. He noticed that every man wore a sword, though few did in the normal course of days, and many leaned on spears and carried their round shields of linden wood rimmed with iron. "What has happened here? What has the priestess to do with this?" A tumult answered him, voices tumbling over each other like brook water over stones.

". . . Burned the farmsteads. . . ."

". . . Men dead, women dead, animals dead. . . ."

". . . Some eaten. . . ."

". . . Devil beast. . . ."

". . . Went to hunt it. . . ."

". . . Ellandune. . . ."

". . . All dead save Godtan. . . ."

"Hold!" Eldran cried. "I cannot hear you all. Who spoke of Ellandune? Is my brother well?"

Silence fell, save for the shuffling of feet. No one would meet his eyes. A murmur spread from the rear of the crowd, and they parted for the passage of a tall woman with a face serene and ageless. Her hair, the black streaked with gray, hung to her ankles and was bound loosely back with a white linen band. Her dress was of pristine linen as well, and the embroideries were of the leaves and berries of the mistletoe. A small golden sickle hung at her belt. She could walk anywhere in Brythunia and the poorest man in the land would not touch that sickle, nor the most violent raise a finger against her.

Eldran's clear gray eyes were troubled as they met hers of dark brown. "Will you tell me, Boudanecea? What has happened to Ellandune?"

"Come with me, Eldran." The priestess took his arm in a strong grasp. "Walk with me, and I will tell you what I can."

He let her lead him away, and none of the rest followed other than with sympathetic eyes that made fear rise in him. In silence they walked slowly down the dusty street. He kept a rein on his impatience, for he knew of old she would not be rushed.

Before the gray stone house where she lived, Boudanecea drew him to a halt. "Go in, Eldran. See Godtan. Speak with him. Then I will tell you."

Eldran hesitated, then pushed open the door of pale polished wood. A short, slight woman met him inside, dressed like Boudanecea, but with her dark, shiny hair braided in tight spirals about her head as a sign that she was still an acolyte.

"Godtan," was all he could say. What of Ellandune, he wanted to shout, but he had begun to fear the answer.

The acolyte silently drew aside a red woolen doorhanging and motioned him to enter the room. A stomach-wrenching melding of smells drifted out. Medicinal herbs and poultices. Burned meat. Rotting meat. He swallowed and ducked through. She let the hanging fall behind him.

It was a simple room, with a well-swept floor of

smooth wooden planks and a single window, its curtains pulled back to admit light. A table with a glazed pottery basin and pitcher stood beside the bed on which lay the naked shape of a man. Or what had once been a man. The right side of his face was burned away, a fringe of gray hair bordering what remained. From the shoulder to the knee· his right side was a mass of charred flesh, crimson showing through cracks in the black. There were no fingers on the twisted stick that had once been his right arm. Eldran remembered that right arm well, for it had taught him the sword.

"Godtan." The name caught in his throat. "Godtan, it is I, Eldran."

The horribly burned man's remaining eye flickered weakly open, swiveled toward him. Eldran groaned at the madness in it.

"We followed," Godtan said, his voice a gurgling croak. "Into—the mountains. Kill it. We were—going to—. We didn't—know. The colors—of it. Beau—tiful. Beautiful—like death. Scales—turned—our arrows—like straws. Spears wouldn't—. Its breath—is fire!"

That mad eye bulged frantically, and Eldran said, "Rest, Godtan. Rest, and I'll—"

"No!" The word came from that twisted mouth with insistence. "No rest! We—fled it. Had to. Hillmen—found us. Took Aelric. Took—Ellandune. Thought—I was—dead. Fooled them." Godtan gave a rasping bark; Eldran realized with a shiver that it was meant to be laughter. "One—of us—had to—

bring word—what happened. I—had to." His one eye swiveled to Eldran's face, and for a moment the madness was replaced by bewilderment and pain. "Forgive—me. I—did not—mean—to leave him. Forgive—Eldran."

"I forgive you," Eldran said softly. "And I thank you for returning with word of what happened. You are still the best man of us all."

A grateful smile curved the half of Godtan's mouth that was left, and his eye drifted shut as if the effort of keeping it open were too great.

Grinding his teeth, Eldran stalked from the building, slapping the door open so that it banged against the wallstones. His eyes were the gray of forged iron, hard and cold from the quenching, and when he confronted Boudanecea his fists were clenched till the nails dug into his palms in an effort to control his anger.

"Will you tell me now?" he grated.

"The beast of fire," she began, but he cut her off.

"A tale for children! Tell me what happened!"

She shook a fist under his nose, and her fury blazed back at him as strongly as his own. "How think you Godtan took his burns? Think, man! A tale for children, you call it. Ha! For all the breadth of your shoulders I've alway had trouble thinking of you as a man grown, for I helped your mother birth you, and wrapped your first swaddling cloths about you with these hands. Now you bring my doubts home again. I know you have the fierce heart of a man. Have you the brain as well?"

Despite his chill rage Eldran was taken aback. He had known Boudanecea since his childhood, and never had he seen her lose her temper. "But, Godtan . . . I thought . . . he's mad."

"Aye, he's mad, and as well he is. All the way from the Kezankians he came, like that, seeking to tell us the fate of his companions, seeking the help of his people. Seeking my help. But none of my spells or potions can help him. The greenrot had set in too deeply by the time I saw him. Only a necromancer could help him now." She touched the golden sickle at her belt to ward off the evil of the thought, and he made the sign of the sickle.

"So the . . . the devil beast came," Eldran said.

Her long hair swayed as she nodded. "While you were in the west. First one farmstead was burned, all of the building, and only gnawed fragments of people or cattle left. Men made up stories to settle their minds, of a fire that killed the family and the animals, of wolves getting at the remains when the fire burned down. But then a second farmstead was destroyed, and a third, and a fourth, and. . . ." She took a long breath. "Twenty-three, in all, and all at night. Seven on the last night alone. After that the hotheads took matters into their own hands. Aelfric. Godtan. Your brother. A score of others. They talked like you when I spoke of the beast of fire after the first farmstead. A tale for children. Then they found spoor, tracks. But they still would not believe me when I said no weapon forged by the hands of ordinary men could harm the creature. They made their plans in secret, and sneaked from the village before dawn to avoid my eye."

"If no weapon forged by man. . . ." Eldran's hands worked futilely. "Boudanecea, I will not let it rest. The hillmen must pay for my brother, and the beast must be slain. Wiccana aid me, it must! Not only for revenge, but to stop it coming again."

"Aye." The priestess breathed the word. "Wait here." In what would have been hurry for one without her stately dignity, she disappeared into her house. When she returned she was followed by a plump acolyte with merry brown eyes. The acolyte carried a flat, red-lacquered chest atop which were neatly folded white cloths and a pitcher of white-glazed pottery. "From this moment," Boudanecea told him, "you must do exactly as you are told, and no more. For your life, Eldran, and your sanity, heed. Now, come."

They formed a procession then, the priestess leading and the acolyte following behind Eldran. The women marched with a measured tread, and he found himself falling into it as if an invisible drum beat the steps.

The hair of the back of his neck stirred as he realized where they were taking him. The Sacred Grove of Wiccana, eldest of the sacred groves of Brythunia, where the boles of the youngest oaks were as thick and as tall as the largest elsewhere in the forest. Only the priestesses and acolytes went to the sacred groves now, though once, countless centuries in the past, men had made that journey. As sacrifices to the goddess. The thought did not comfort Eldran.

Limbs as thick as a man's body wove a canopy
above their heads, and the decaying leaves of the past
season rustled beneath their feet. Abruptly a clearing
appeared before them, where a broad, low grassy
mound lay bare to the sky. A rough slab of granite,
as long and as wide as the height of a man, lay
partially buried in the side of the mound before them.

"Attempt to move the stone," Boudanecea commanded.

Eldran stared at her. He was head and shoulders
taller than most men of the village, well muscled and
with broad shoulders, but he knew the weight was
beyond him. Then, remembering her first instructions,
he obeyed. Squatting beside the great stone, he tried
to dig down with his hands to find the lower edge.
The first handfuls moved easily, but abruptly the dirt
took on the consistency of rock. It looked no different than before, yet his nails could not scratch it.
Giving up on that, he threw his weight against the
side of the slab, attempting to lever it over. Every
sinew of him strained, and sweat ran in rivulets down
his face and body, but the granite seemed a fixed part
of the mound. It did not stir.

"Enough," Boudanecea said. "Come and kneel
here." She indicated a spot before the slab.

The acolyte had laid open the top of the chest,
revealing stoppered vials and bowls of a glaze that
seemed the exact green of mistletoe. Boudanecea
firmly turned Eldran's back to the plump woman and
made him kneel. From the white pitcher she poured
clear water over his hands, and wiped them with soft

white cloths. Other cloths were dampened and used to wipe sweat from his face.

As she cleansed his face and hands the graying priestess spoke. "No man or woman can move that stone, nor enter that mound save with Wiccana's aid. *With* her aid. . . ."

The acolyte appeared at her side, holding a small green bowl. With her golden sickle Boudacenea cut a lock of Eldran's hair. He shivered as she dropped it into the bowl. Taking each of his hands in turn, she pricked the balls of his thumbs with the point of the sickle and squeezed a few drops of his blood on top of the hair. The acolyte and bowl hurried from his view again.

Boudanecea's eyes held his. He could hear the plump woman clinking vials, murmuring incantations, but he could not look away from the priestess' face. Then the acolyte was back, and Boudanecea took from her the bowl and a long sprig of mistletoe, which she dipped into the bowl.

Head back, the priestess began to chant. The words she spoke were no words Eldran had ever heard before, but the power of them chilled him to the bone. The air about him became icy and still. A thrill of terror went through him as he held out his hands, palms up, without instruction. It was as if he suddenly had known that he must do it. Mistletoe slapped his hands, and terror was replaced by a feeling of wholeness and wellbeing greater than any he had ever known before. Boudanecea chanted on, her paean rising in tone. The dampened sprig of mistletoe struck one cheek, then the other. Abruptly his body seemed to have no weight; he felt as if he might drift on the lightest breeze.

Boudanecea's voice stilled. Eldran wavered, then staggered to his feet. The peculiar sense of lightness remained with him.

"Go to the stone." Boudanecea's voice hung like chimes in the crystallized air. "Move the stone aside."

Silently Eldran moved to the slab. It had not changed that he could see, and rather than feeling stronger, he seemed to have no strength at all. Still the compulsion of her words was on him. Bending beside the stone, he fitted his hands to it, heaved . . . and his mouth fell open as the stone rose like a feather, pivoted on its further edge, and fell soundlessly. He stared at the stone, at his hands, at the sloping passage revealed in the side of the mound, at Boudanecea.

"Go down," she told him. Tension froze her face, and insistence made her words ring more loudly. "Go down, and bring back what you find."

Taking a deep breath, Eldran stumbled down the slanting, dirt-floored passage. No dust rose beneath his feet. Broad, long slabs of stone had been carefully laid for walls and roof to the passage, their crude work showing their age. Quickly the passage widened into a round chamber, some ten paces across, walled and roofed in the same gray stone as the way down. There were no lamps, but a soft light permeated the room. Nor were there the cobwebs and dust he had expected. A smell of freshly grown green things hung in the air, a smell of spring.

There could be no doubt as to what he was to bring up, for the chamber was bare save for a simple pedestal of pale stone, atop which rested a sword of ancient design. Its broad blade gleamed brightly, as if it had just come, newly made and freshly oiled, from the smith's hand. The bronze hilt was wrapped with leather that could have have been tanned that season. Its quillons ended in claws that seemed designed to hold something, but they were empty now.

A sense of urgency came on him as he stared at the sword. Seizing it, he half-ran back to the sunlight above.

As he took his first step onto the ground of the clearing he heaved a sigh of relief. And suddenly he felt as he had before coming there. All the strange sensations were gone. Almost against his will he looked over his shoulder. The great stone rested where it had originally lain, with no sign that it had ever been disturbed. Even the place where he had dug beside it was no longer there.

A shudder ran down his bones. Only the weight of the sword in his hand—an ordinary seeming, if ancient, blade—remained to convince him something had actually happened. He clung hard to sanity, and did not wonder about what that something had been.

"Flame Slayer," Boudanecea said softly. Her hand stretched toward the sword, but did not touch it. "Symbol of our people, sword of our people's heroes. It was forged by great wizards nearly three thousand years ago, as a weapon against the beasts of fire, for the evil of Acheron had launched a plague of them, creations of their vile sorceries, upon the world. Once those claws held two great rubies, the Eyes of Fire, and the sword could control the beasts as well as slay them. For it *can* slay the beast.''

"Why didn't you tell me of it?" Eldran demanded. "Why did you bring me here unknowing, like a sheep to. . . .'' His voice trailed off, for he did not like the thoughts that image brought back.

"It is part of the *geas* laid on the sword," the priestess replied, "and on we who keep it. Without the aid of a priestess, no one can reach the sword. But no priestess may speak of the sword to any who does not hold it. Great care must be taken in choosing to bring a man to the blade, for as well as its uses against the beasts of fire it can be a locus of great power to one who knows the ways of such things.''

He hefted the sword curiously. "Power? Of what kind?''

"Do you seek power, Eldran?" she asked gravely. "Or do you seek to slay the beast?''

"The beast," he growled, and she nodded approval.

"Good. I chose you when first I knew what the beast was. You are acknowledged the finest man in Brythunia with sword or horse or bow. It is said that you move through the forest, and the trees are unaware of your passage, that you can track the wind itself. Such a man will be needed to hunt down the beast of fire. And this you must remember. Do not allow the sword to leave your possession, even while you sleep, or you will never regain its hilt. Instead the sword will, Wiccana alone knows how, return to its place beneath the stone. Many times it has been lost, but always, when it is needed and the stone is lifted aside, the sword is there. That will not help you should you lose it, though, for the sword may be given to any man but once in his life.''

"I will not lose it," Eldran said grimly. "It will do its work, and I will return it here myself. But now I must take it from here.'' He began to move toward the trees, out of the sacred grove; his first nervousness was returning, as if this was not a place for men to remain long. ''There is no time to waste, so I must choose the rest of my party quickly.''

''Rest?'' Boudanecea exclaimed, halting him at the edge of the trees. ''I intended you to go alone, one swift hunter to slay the—''

"No. There must be blood price for Aelric and Ellandune, and for any others who fell to the hillmen. You know it must be so.''

"I know," she sighed. "Your mother was like my own sister. I had hoped to hold her grandson one day, hoped for it many a day before this. Now I fear I never shall.''

"I will come back," he said, and laughed suddenly, shocking himself. ''You will get to see me wed yet, Boudanecea.''

She raised the mistletoe in benediction, and he bowed his head to accept it. But even as he did he was listing in his mind the men he would take into the mountains with him.

Chapter 9

Easing himself in his high-pommeled Zamoran saddle, Conan studied the country toward which the hunting party traveled. The flat, rolling hills through which they rode had changed little in the three days since his rescue of Jondra, except that the short grass was more abundant here and a brown tangle of thornbushes occasionally covered a stony slope. Ahead, though, the hills rose quickly higher, piling up on one another till they melded into the jagged, towering peaks of the Kezankians.

These were an arm of that range that stretched south and west along the border between Zamora and Brythunia. Conan knew of no game in them that would attract a hunter like Jondra save for the great spiral-horned sheep that lived amid the sheer cliffs in the heart of the range. In the heart of the mountain tribes, as well. He could not believe she meant to venture there.

The hunting party was a vile-tempered snake twisting its way among the low hills, avoiding the crests. Spearmen muttered oaths as their sandaled feet slipped on stony slopes, exchanging insults with mounted archers. Pack animals brayed and muleteers cursed. Ox drivers shouted and cracked their long whips as the oxen strained to pull the high-wheeled supply carts. The string of spare horses, raising an even taller plume of dust than all the rest of the party, was the only part of the column not adding to the tumult. Jondra rode before it all with Arvaneus and half a score other mounted hunters, oblivious of the noise behind them. It was no way to enter the country of the hill tribes. Conan was only thankful the dogs had been left behind in Shadizar.

Tamira, perched precariously atop lashed bundles of tenting on a lurching cart, waved to him, and Conan moved his horse up beside the cart. "You surprise me," he said. "You have avoided me these three days past."

"The Lady Jondra finds many labors for me," she replied. Eying the carter, walking beside his oxen, she edged more to the rear of the high-wheeled vehicle. "Why did you follow me?" she whispered fiercely.

Conan smiled lazily. "Followed you? Perhaps I seek the country air. Invigorating rides are good for the lungs, I'm told."

"Invigorating—" She spluttered indignantly. "Tell me the truth, Cimmerian! If you think to cut me out—"

"Already I have told you my plans for you," he broke in.

"You . . . you are serious?" she said, a rising note of incredulity in her voice. As if fearing he might seize her on the instant, she wiggled to the far side of the cart and peered at him over the top of the rolled tenting. "The Lady Jondra requires that her handmaidens be chaste, Cimmerian. You may think that saving her life will gain you license, but she is a noble, and will forget her gratitude in a moment if you transgress her rules."

"Then I will have to be careful, won't I?" Conan said, letting his horse fall behind. She peered after him anxiously as the cart trundled on. Conan wore a satisfied smile.

He was sure she did not believe that he had no interest in Jondra's jewels—she was no fool, or she could not have thieved as long as she had in Shadizar—but she would at least think his mind was divided between the gems and her. Most women, he had found, would believe that a man lusted after them on the slightest provocation. And if Tamira believed that, she would be nervously looking over her shoulder when she should be getting her hands on the gems.

A blackened hillside caught the big Cimmerian's eye, off from the line of march, and he turned his horse aside from curiosity. Nothing was left of the thornbushes that had once covered the slope save charred stumps and ashes. It did not have the look of lightning strike, he thought, for the bolt would have struck the hilltop, not its side.

Abruptly his mount stopped, nostrils flaring, and gave a low, fearful whicker. Conan tried to urge the animal closer, but it refused, even taking a step back. He frowned, unable to see anything ominous. What would frighten a horse he had been told was trained for the hunting of lions?

Dismounting, he dropped his reins, then watched to be sure the animal would stand. Its flanks shivered, but training held it. Satisfied, Conan approached the burn. And loosened his sword, just in case.

At first his booted feet stirred only ashes over blackened soil and rock. Then his toe struck something different. He picked up a broken wild ox horn with a fragment of skull attached. The horn was charred, as were the shreds of flesh adhering to the bone, but the piece of skull itself was not. Slowly he searched through the entire burn. There were no other bones to be found, not even such cracked bits as hyenas would leave after scavenging a lion's kill. He extended his search to the area around the char.

With a clatter of hooves Arvaneus galloped up, working his reins to make his horse dance as he stared down at Conan. "If you fall behind, barbar," the hawk-faced man said contemptuously, "you may not be so lucky as to find others to take you in."

Conan's hands tightened on the horn. The gems, he reminded himself firmly. "I found this in the ashes, and—"

"An old ox horn," the huntsman snorted, "and a lightning strike. No doubt it signifies some portent to one such as you, but we have no time for wasting."

Taking a deep breath, Conan went on. ''There are tracks—''

''I have trackers, barbar. I have no need of you. Better you do fall behind. Leave us, barbar, while you can.'' Wheeling his mount in a spray of rocks and dirt, Arvaneus galloped after the fast-disappearing column.

There was a sharp crack, and Conan discovered that the ox horn had broken in his grip. ''Zandru's Nine Hells!'' he muttered.

Tossing the shattered remnants of horn aside, he knelt to examine the track he had found. It was only part of an animal's print, for the stony soil did not take tracks well. At least, he thought it was an animal's print. Two toes ending in long claws, and scuffings that might have indicated the rest of the foot. He laid a forefinger beside one of the claw marks. The claw had been easily twice as large as his finger.

He had never heard of a beast that made tracks as large as these. At least, he thought, Jondra did not hunt this. Nor did he think he would warn her of it. What he knew of her suggested she would leap at the chance to hunt an unknown creature, especially if it was dangerous. Still, he would keep his own eyes open. Swinging into the saddle, he galloped after the hunting party.

Sooner than Conan expected, he caught up with them. The column was halted. Men held the horses' heads to keep them silent, and the carters held the oxen's nose-rings so they would not low. Tamira paused in beating dust from her short white tunic to grimace at Conan as he walked his horse past the cart of tenting. From somewhere ahead came a faint, steady pounding of drums.

At the front of the line Jondra and a handful of her hunters lay on their bellies near the crest of a hill. Leaving his horse at the foot of the slope, Conan made his way up to them, dropping flat before his head overtopped the hill. The drumbeat was louder here.

"Go, barbar," Arvaneus snarled. "You are not needed here."

"Be silent, Arvaneus," Jondra said softly, but there was iron in her tone.

Conan ignored them both. A third of a league distant another column marched, this one following a knife-edge line, caring not whether it topped hills or no. A column of the Zamoran Army. Ten score horsemen in spiked helms rode in four files behind a leopard-head standard. Behind came twenty drummers, mallets rising and falling in unison, and behind them. . . . The Cimmerian made a rough estimate of the numbers of sloped spears, rank on rank on rank. Five thousand Zamoran infantry made a drum of the ground with their measured tread.

Conan turned his head to gaze at Jondra. Color came into her cheeks beneath his eyes. "Why do you avoid the army?" he asked.

"We will camp," Jondra said. "Find a site, Arvaneus." She began moving backwards down the slope, and the huntsman slithered after her.

Conan watched them go with a frown, then turned back to peer after the soldiers until they had marched out of sight beyond the hills to the north.

The camp was set up when Conan finally left the hill, conical tents dotting a broad, flat space between two hills. Jondra's large tent of bright scarlet stood in the center of the area. The oxen had been hobbled, and the horses tied along a picket line beyond the carts. No fires were lit, he noted, and the cooks were handing out dried meat and fruit.

"You, barbar," Arvaneus said around a strip of jerky. "I see you waited until the work was done before coming in."

"Why does Jondra avoid the army?" Conan demanded.

The hawk-faced man spit out a wad of half-chewed meat. "The *Lady* Jondra," he snapped. "Show a proper respect toward her, barbar, or I'll. . . ." His hand clutched the hilt of his tulwar.

A slow smile appeared on Conan's face, a smile that did not extend to suddenly steely eyes. There were dead men who could have told Arvaneus about that smile. "What, huntsman? Try what is in your mind, if you think you are man enough." In an instant the black-eyed man's curved blade was bare, and, though Conan's hand had not been near his sword hilt, his broadsword was out in the same breath.

Arvaneus blinked, taken aback at the big Cimmerian's quickness. "Do you know who I am, barbar?" There was a shakiness to his voice, and his face tightened at it. "Huntsman, you call me, but I am the son of Lord Andanezeus, and if she who bore me had not been a concubine I would be a lord of Zamora. Noble blood flows in my veins, barbar, blood fit for the Lady Jondra herself, while yours is—''

"Arvaneus!" Jondra's voice cracked like a whip over the camp. Pale faced, the noblewoman came to within a pace of the two men. Her close-fitting leather jerkin was laced tightly up the front, and red leather boots rose to her knees. Arvaneus watched her with a tortured expression on his face. Her troubled gray eyes touched Conan's face, then jerked away. "You overstep yourself, Arvaneus," she said unsteadily. "Put up your sword." Her eyes flickered to Conan. "Both of you."

Arvaneus' face was a mosaic of emotion, rage and shame, desire and frustration. With a wordless shout he slammed his blade back into its scabbard as if into the tall Cimmerian's ribs.

Conan waited until the other's sword was covered before sheathing his own, then said grimly, "I still want to know why you hide from your own army."

Jondra looked at him, hesitating, but Arvaneus spoke up quickly, urgently. "My lady, this man should not be among us. He is no hunter, no archer or spearman. He does not serve you as . . . as I do."

With a deep chuckle, Conan shook his black-maned head. "It is true I am my own man, but I am as good a hunter as you, Zamoran. And as for the spear, will you match me at it? For coin?" He knew he must best the man at something, or else contend with him as long as he remained with the hunters. And he carefully had not mentioned the bow, of which he knew little beyond the holding of it.

"Done!" the huntsman cried. "Done! Bring the butts! Quickly! I will show this barbarian oaf the way of the spear!"

Jondra opened her mouth as if to speak, then closed it again as the camp erupted in a bustle of men, some scurrying to clear a space for the throwing, others rushing to the carts to wrestle with a heavy practice butt. The thick bundle woven of straw was a weighty burden to carry on a hunting expedition, but it did not break arrows or spear points, as did casting and shooting at trees or at targets on a hillside.

A shaven-headed man with a long nose leaped on an upturned keg. "I'll cover all wagers! I give one to twenty on Arvaneus, twenty to one on the barbarian. Don't crowd." A few men wandered over to him, but most seemed to take the outcome as foregone.

Conan noticed Tamira among those about the keg. When she left she strolled by him. "Throw your best," she said, "and I'll win a silver piece. . . ." She waited until his chest began to expand with pride, then finished with a laugh, ". . . Since I wagered on the other."

"It will be a pleasure to help you lose your coppers," he told her dryly.

"Stop flirting, Lyana," Jondra called sharply. "There's work for you to be doing."

Tamira made a face the tall woman could not see,

bringing a smile to Conan's face despite himself, then scurried away.

"Will you throw, barbar?" Arvaneus asked tauntingly. The tall huntsman held a spear in his hand and was stripped to the waist, revealing hard ropes of muscle. "Or would you rather stay with the serving girl?"

"The girl is certainly more pleasing to look on than your face," Conan replied.

Arvaneus' face darkened at the ripple of laughter that greeted the Cimmerian's words. With the blade of his spear the Zamoran scratched a line on the ground. "No part of your foot may pass this line, or you lose no matter how well you throw. Though I doubt I must worry about that."

Doffing his tunic, Conan took a spear handed to him by another of the hunters and moved to the line. He eyed the butt, thirty paces away. "It does not look a great distance."

"But see the target, barbar." The swarthy huntsman smiled, pointing. A lanky spearman was just finishing attaching a circle of black cloth, no bigger than a man's palm, to the straw.

Conan made his eyes go wide. "Aaah," he breathed, and the hawk-faced man's smile deepened.

"To be fair," Arvaneus announced loudly, "I will give you odds. One hundred to one." A murmur rose among the watchers, and all in the camp were there. "You did mention coin, barbar. Unless you wish to acknowledge me the better man now."

"They seem fair odds," Conan said, "considering

the reputation you have with yourself.'' The murmur of astonishment at the odds offered became a roar of laughter. He considered the weight of his purse. ''I have five silver pieces at those odds.'' The laughter cut off in stunned silence. Few there thought the hawk-faced man might lose, but the sheer magnitude of his unlikely loss astounded them.

Arvaneus seemed unmoved. ''Done,'' was all he said. He moved back from the line, took two quick steps forward, and hurled. His spear streaked to the center of the black cloth, pinning it more firmly to the butt. Half a score of the hunters raised a cheer, and some began trying to collect their bets now. ''Done,'' he said again, and laughed mockingly.

Conan hefted his spear as he stood at the line. The haft was as thick as his two thumbs, tipped with an iron blade as long as his forearm. Suddenly he leaned back, then whipped forward, arm and body moving as one. With a thud that shoved the butt back his spear buried its head not a finger's width from the other already there. ''Mayhap if it were further back,'' he mused. Arvaneus ground his teeth.

There was silence in the camp till the man on the keg broke it. ''Even odds! I'll give even odds on Arvaneus or—what's his name? Conan?—or on Conan! Even odds!''

''Shut your teeth, Telades!'' Arvaneus shouted, but men crowded around the shaven-headed man. Angrily the huntsman gestured toward the butt. ''Back! Move it back!'' Two men rushed out to drag it a further ten paces, then returned quickly with the spears.

Glaring at Conan, Arvaneus took his place back from the line again, ran forward and threw. Again his spear struck through the cloth. Conan stepped back a single pace, and again his throw was one single continuous motion. His spear brushed against Arvaneus's, striking through the black cloth even more closely than the first time. Scattered shouts of delighted surprise rose among the hunters. The Cimmerian was surprised to see a smile on Jondra's face, and even more surprised to see another on Tamira's.

Arvaneus's face writhed with fury. "Further!" he shouted when the spears were returned once more. "Further! Still further!"

An expectant hush settled as the butt was pulled to sixty paces distant. It was a fair throw for the mark, Conan conceded to himself. Perhaps more than a fair throw.

Muttering under his breath, the huntsman set himself, then launched his spear with a grunt. It smacked home solidly in the butt.

"A miss!" Telades called. "It touched the cloth, but a miss! One to five on Conan!"

Arm cocked, Conan hurtled toward the line. For the third time his shaft streaked a dark line to the cloth. A tumultuous cry went up, and men pounded their spears on the ground in approbation.

Telades leaped from his keg and capered laughing through the crowd to clasp Conan's hand. "You've cost me coin this day, northerner, but 'twas worth every copper to see it done.''

Eyes bulging in his head, Arvaneus gave a strangled cry. "No!" Suddenly he was running toward the butt, pushing men from his path. He began wrestling the heavy mass of straw further away. "Hit this, barbar dog!" he shouted, fighting his weighty burden still. "Erlik take you and your accursed cheating tricks! Hit this!"

"Why, 'tis a hundred paces," Telades exclaimed, shaking his head. "No man could—" He cut off with a gasp as Conan took a spear from the hand of a nearby hunter. Like antelope scattering before a lion, men ran to get from between the Cimmerian and the distant target.

Arvaneus' voice drifted back to them, filled with hysterical laughter. "Hit this, barbar! Try!"

Weighing the spear in his hand, Conan suddenly moved. Powerful legs drove him forward, his arm went back, and the spear arched high into the air. The hawk-faced huntsman stared open-mouthed at the spear arcing toward him, then screamed and hurled himself aside. Dust lifted from the butt as the spear slashed into the straw beside the two already there.

Telades ran forward, peering in disbelief, then whirled to throw his arms high. "By all the gods, he hit cloth! You who call yourselves spearmen, acknowledge your master! At a hundred paces he hit the cloth!"

A throng of hunters crowded around Conan, shouting their approval of his feat, striving to clasp his hand.

Abruptly the shouts faded as Jondra strode up. The hunters parted before her, waiting expectantly for what she would say. For a moment, though, she stood, strangely diffident, before speaking.

"You asked me a question, Cimmerian," she said at last, looking over his shoulder rather than at him. "I do not give reasons for what I do, but you *did* save my life, and your cast was magnificent, so I will tell you alone. But in private. Come." Back rigid and looking neither to left nor right, she turned and walked to her scarlet tent.

Conan followed more slowly. When he ducked through the tent flap, the well-curved noblewoman stood with her back to the entrance, toying with the laces of her leather jerkin. Fine Iranistani carpets, dotted with silken pillows, made a floor, and golden lamps stood on low, brass tables.

"Why, then?" he said.

She started, but did not turn around. "If the army is out in such force," she said distractedly, "they must expect trouble of some sort. They would surely try to turn back a hunting party, and I do not want the trouble of convincing some general that I will not be ordered about by the army."

"And you keep this secret?" Conan said, frowning. "Do you think your hunters have not reasoned some of this out themselves?"

"Is Lyana as you said?" she asked. "Pleasing to look on? More pleasing than I?"

"She is lovely." Conan smiled at the stiffening of her back, and added judiciously, "But not so lovely as you." He was young, but he knew enough of women to take care in speaking of one woman's beauty to another.

"I will pay Arvaneus's wager," Jondra said abruptly. "He does not have five hundred pieces of silver."

The tall Cimmerian blinked, taken aback by her sudden shift. "I will not take it from you. The wager was with him."

Her head bowed, and she muttered, seemingly unaware that she spoke aloud. "Why is he always the same in my mind? Why must he be a barbarian?" Suddenly she turned, and Conan gasped. She had worked the laces from her jerkin, and the supple leather gaped open to bare heavy, round breasts and erect, pink nipples. "Did you think I brought you to my tent merely to answer your questions?" she cried. "I've allowed no man to touch me, but you will not even stretch out a hand. Will you make me be as shameless as—"

The young noblewoman's words cut off as Conan pulled her to him. His big hands slid beneath her jerkin, fingers spreading on the smooth skin of her back, to press her full breasts against him. "I stretch out both hands," he said, working the leather from her shoulders to fall to the carpets.

Clutching at him, she laid her head against his broad chest. "My hunters will know . . . they will guess what I . . . what you. . . ." She shivered and held to him harder.

Gently he tipped her head back and peered into her eyes, as gray as the clouds of a mountain morning. "If you fear what they think," he said, "then why?"

The tip of her small pink tongue wet her lips. "I could never have made that spear cast," she murmured, and pulled him down to the silken cushions.

Chapter 10

Conan tossed aside the fur coverlet and got to his feet with an appreciative look at Jondra's nude form. She sighed in her sleep, and threw her arms over her head, tightening the domes of her breasts in such a way as to make him consider not dressing after all. Chuckling, he reached for his tunic instead. The locked iron chests containing her gems got not a wit of his attention.

Three days since the spear casting, he reflected, and for all her fears of what her hunters might think, it would take a man both blind and deaf to be still unaware of what occurred between Jondra and him. She had not let him leave her tent that first night, not even to eat, and the past two had been the same. Each morning, seemingly oblivious of the hunters' smiles and Arvaneus's glares, she insisted that Conan "guide" her while she hunted, a hunt that lasted only until she found a spot well away from the line of march where there was shade and a level surface

large enough for two. The chaste, noble Lady Jondra
had found that she liked lying with a man, and she
was making up for lost opportunities.

Not that her absorbtion in the flesh was total. That
first day she had been unsatisfied on their return with
how far the column had traveled. Up and down the
line she galloped, scoring men with her tongue till
they were as shaken as if she had used her quirt.
Arvaneus she took aside, and what she said to him no
one heard, but when he galloped back his lips were a
tight, pale line, and his black eyes smouldered. There
had not been another day when the progress of the
column failed to satisfy her.

Settling his black Khauranian cloak around his
shoulders, Conan stepped out into the cool morning.
He was pleased to see that the cookfires had at last
been made with dried ox dung, as he had suggested.
No smoke rose to draw eyes to them, and that was
more important than ever, now. A day to the north of
where they camped, at most two days amid the now
steep-sloped hills, lay the towering ranges of the
Kezankian, dark and jagged against the horizon.

The camp itself squatted atop a hill amidst trees
twisted and stunted by arid, rocky soil. Every man
wore his mail shirt and spiked helm at all times,
now, and none went so far as the privy trenches
without spear or bow.

A sweating Tamira, dodging from fire to fire under
the watchful eye of the fat cook, gave Conan a
grimace as she twisted a meat-laden spit half a turn.
Arvaneus, sitting cross-legged near the fires, sullenly

buried his face in a mug of wine when he saw the Cimmerian.

Conan ignored them both. His ears strained for the sound he thought he had heard. There. He grabbed Tamira's arm. "Go wake J . . . your mistress," he told her. Hands on hips, Tamira stared at him wryly. "Go," he growled. "There are horsemen coming from the south." A look of startlement passed over her face, then she darted for the big scarlet tent.

"What offal do you spout now?" Arvaneus demanded. "I see nothing."

Telades came running across the camp to the hawk-faced man's side. "Mardak claims he hears horses to the south, Arvaneus."

With an oath the huntsman tossed his mug to the ground and scrambled to his feet. A worried frown creased his face. "Hillmen?" he asked Telades, and the shaven-headed man shrugged.

"Not likely from the south," Conan said. "Still, it couldn't hurt to let the rest of the camp know. Quietly."

"When I need your advice," Arvaneus snarled, but he did not finish it. Instead he turned to Telades. "Go among the men. Tell them to be ready." His face twitched, and he added a muttered, "Quietly."

Unasked, the Cimmerian added his efforts to those of Telades, moving from man to man, murmuring a word of warning. Mardak, a grizzled, squint-eyed man with long, thin mustaches also was passing the word. The hunters took it calmly. Here and there a man fingered the hilt of his tulwar or pulled a lacquered quiver of arrows closer, but all went on with what they were doing, though with eyes continually flickering to the south.

By the time Conan returned to the center of the camp, ten horsemen had topped the crest of the next hill and were walking their horses toward the camp.

Arvaneus grunted. "We could slay all of them before they knew we were here. What are they, anyway? Not hillmen."

"Brythunians," Telades replied. "Is there really cause to kill them, Arvaneus?"

"Barbarian scum," the hawk-faced hunter sneered. "They don't even see us."

"They see us," Conan said, "or they'd never have crossed that crest. And what makes you think we see all of them?"

The two Zamorans exchanged surprised looks, but Conan concentrated on the oncoming men. All wore fur leggings and fur-edged capes, with broadswords at their waists and round shields hung behind their saddles. Nine of them carried spears. One, who led them, carried a long, recurved bow.

The Brythunian horsemen picked their way up the hill and drew rein short of the camp. The man with the bow raised it above his head. "I am called Eldran," he said. "Are we welcome here?"

A sour look on his face, Arvaneus stood silent.

Conan raised his right hand above his head. "I am called Conan," he said. "I welcome you, so long as you mean harm to none here. Dismount and share our fires."

Eldran climbed from his horse with a smile. He was almost as tall as Conan, though not so heavily muscled. "We cannot remain long. We seek information, then we must move on."

"I seek information as well," Jondra said as she strode between the men. Her hair, light brown sun-streaked with blonde, was tousled, and her tight riding breeches and tunic of emerald silk had an air of having been hastily donned. "Tell me. . . ." Her words died as her eyes met those of Eldran, as gray as her own. Her head was tilted back to look up at him, and her mouth remained open. Finally she said unsteadily, "From . . . from what country are you?"

"They're Brythunians," Arvaneus spoke up. "Savages."

"Be silent!" Jondra's enraged scream caught the men by surprise. Conan and Eldran stared at her wonderingly. Arvaneus's face paled. "I did not speak to you," she went on in a voice that shook. "You will be silent till spoken to! Do you understand me, huntsman?" Not waiting for his answer, she turned back to Eldran. The color in her cheeks was high, her voice thin but cool. "You are hunters, then? It is doubly dangerous for you to hunt here. The Zamoran army is in the field, and there are always the hillmen."

"The Zamoran army does not seem to find us," the Brythunian answered. His still-mounted men laughed. "As for the hillmen. . . ." There was an easiness to his voice, but grim light flashed in his eyes. "I have given my name, woman, but have not heard yours."

She drew herself up to her greatest height, still no taller than his shoulder. "It is the Lady Jondra of the House Perashanid of Shadizar, to whom you speak, Brythunian."

"An honorable lineage, Zamoran."

His tone was neutral, but Jondra flinched as if he had sneered. Strangely, it seemed to steady her in some fashion. Her voice firmed. "If you are a hunter, perhaps you have seen the beast I hunt, or its sign. I am told its body is that of a huge serpent, covered with scales in many colors. Its track—"

"The beast of fire," one of the mounted Brythunians murmured, and others made a curving sign in the air before them as if it were a charm.

Eldran's face was tight. "We seek the beast as well, Jondra. Our people know it of old. Perhaps we can join forces."

"I need no more hunters," Jondra said quickly.

"The creature is more difficult to slay than you can imagine," the tall Brythunian said urgently. His hand gripped tightly at the hilt of his sword, a weapon of ancient pattern with quillons ending in claws like an eagle's. "It's breath is fire. Without us you can but die in the seeking of it."

"So say you," she said mockingly, "with your children's tales. I say I will slay the beast, and without your aid. I also say that I had better not find you attempting to poach my kill. This trophy is mine, Brythunian. Do you understand me?"

"Your eyes are like the mists of dawn," he said, smiling.

Jondra quivered. "If I see you again, I'll put arrows in both of *your* eyes. I'll—"

Suddenly she grabbed a bow from one of her archers. Brythunian spears were lowered, and their horses pranced nervously. Hunters reached for their tulwars. In one smooth motion Jondra drew and released, into the air. Far above the camp a raven gave a shrill cry and began to flutter erratically, dropping toward a far hill.

"See that," Jondra exclaimed, "and fear my shafts."

Before the words were out of her mouth the distant raven jerked downward, turning over as it plummeted to reveal a second arrow transfixing its feathered corpse.

"You are a fine shot," Eldran said as he lowered his bow. Smoothly he swung into his saddle. "I would stay to shoot with you, but I have hunting to do." Without a backward glance he wheeled his horse and rode down the hill, his men following as if unaware that their backs were bare to the camp's archers.

That thought occurred quickly to Arvaneus. "Archers," he began, when Jondra whirled on him, glaring. She said no word, nor needed to. The huntsman backed away from her, eyes down, muttering, "Your forgiveness, my lady."

Next she turned her attentions to Conan. "You," she breathed. "He spoke to me like that, and you did nothing. Nothing!"

The big Cimmerian eyed her impassively. "Perhaps

he is right. I found signs of a beast that may kill with fire. And if he is right about that, perhaps he is right about the difficulty of killing it. Perhaps you should return to Shadizar.''

''Perhaps, perhaps, perhaps!'' She spat each word. ''Why was I not told of these signs? Arvaneus, what do you know of this?''

The huntsman darted a malice-filled gaze at Conan. ''A fire begun by lightning,'' he said sullenly, ''and a few old bones. This one is frightened by his own shadow. Or by the shadow of the mountains.''

''That is not true, is it?'' Jondra's eyes were doubtful on Conan's face. ''You do not make invention for fear of dying at the hillmen's hands, do you?''

''I do not fear death,'' Conan said flatly. ''The dark will come when it comes. But none save a fool seeks it out needlessly.''

The noblewoman tossed her head haughtily. ''So,'' she said, and again, ''So.'' Without another look at Conan, she stalked away, calling loudly, ''Lyana! Prepare my morning bath, girl!''

Arvaneus grinned at Conan malevolently, but the Cimmerian youth did not see him. Matters had become complex far beyond his simple plans on leaving Shadizar, Conan thought. What was he to do now? There was one way he knew to concentrate his mind for the solution of a problem. Producing a small whetstone from his pouch, he drew his sword and settled cross-legged to touch up the edge on the ancient blade and think.

*   *   *

Basrakan Imalla glared at the raven lying dead on his chamber floor and tugged at the forks of his beard in frustration. The watch-ravens were not easily come by. Nestlings must be secured, and only one pair in twenty survived the incantations that linked them so that one of the two saw and experienced what the other did. Time to secure the birds, time to work the spells. He had no time for replacing the accursed bird. Likely the other had fallen to a hawk. And he had so few of them.

With a grunt he kicked the dead bird, smashing it into the bare stone wall. "Filthy creature," he snarled.

Tugging his crimson robes straight, he turned to the six tall perches that stood in the center of the floor. On five of the perches ravens sat, tilting their heads to watch him with eyes like shiny black beads. Their wings, clipped so they could not fly, drooped listlessly. There were few furnishings in the room other than those perches. A table inlaid with mother-of-pearl bore a brass lamp and a scattering of implements for the dark arts. A shelf along one wall held the volumes of necromantic lore that he had gathered in a lifetime. No one entered that room, or the others reserved to his great work, save him, and none save his acolytes knew what occurred there.

Lighting a splinter of wood at the lamp, Basrakan began to trace an intricate figure in the air before the first bird. The tiny eyes followed the flame, which was mirrored in their black surfaces. As he traced, Basrakan chanted words from a tome copied on vellum made of human skin rather than sheepskin, words that floated in the air till the walls seemed to shimmer. With each word the tracing grew more solid, till an unholy symbol in fire hung between himself and the raven.

The raven's beak opened with painful slowness, and creaking words, barely recognizable, emerged. "Hills. Sky. Trees. Clouds. Many many clouds."

The sorcerer clapped his hands; the fiery image vanished, and the words ceased to come. It was often thus with the creatures. By the spells that held them they would speak of men before all else, but if there were no men they would mutter about whatever they happened to see, go on forever if he did not silence them.

The same ritual before the next bird gained him the same reply, with only the terrain changed, as did the next and the next. By the time he reached the last raven he was hurrying. An important matter awaited his attention in the next room, and he was certain by now what the creature would report. Chanting, he traced the symbol in fire, preparing even as it came into being to clap his hands.

"Soldiers," the raven croaked. "Many many. Many many."

Barakan's breath caught in his throat. Never more than now had he regretted the inability of the ravens to transmit numbers. "Where?" he demanded.

"South. South of mountains."

Thoughtfully the stern-faced Imalla stroked his beard. If they came from the south, they must be Zamorans. But how to deal with them? The bird that had actually seen the soldiers could be made to return and guide his warriors back to them. The men would see it as a further sign of the favor of the old gods, for birds were creatures of the spirits of the air. And it would the first victory, the first of many against the unbelievers.

"Return!" Basrakan commanded.

"Return," the raven croaked agreement, and he broke the link.

How many soldiers, he wondered as he strode from the chamber, and how many warriors of the true gods to send against them?

As he passed through the next chamber, he paused to ponder the girl who cowered against a wall paneled in polished oak, as rare and costly in these mountains as pearls. Her dark eyes streamed tears, and her full mouth quivered uncontrollably. Her skin was smooth and supple, and his view of it was not hampered by garments.

Basrakan grimaced in disgust and wiped his hands on the front of his scarlet robes. Only eighteen, and already she was a vessel of lust, attempting to ensnare the minds of men. As did all women. None were truly pure. None were worthy of the ancient gods.

Shaking himself from his dark reverie, the holy man hurried on. He had no fear for the girl's wandering. The *geas* he had put on her would not allow her to leave that chamber until he gave her permission, until he found her worthy.

In the corridor he found Jbeil Imalla just entering his abode. The lean man bowed, his black robes rustling stiffly. "The blessings of the true gods be on you, Basrakan Imalla. I come with ill tidings."

"Ill tidings?" Basrakan said, ignoring the greeting. "Speak, man!"

"Many warriors have joined our number, but most of them have never seen the sign of the true gods' favor." Jbeil's dark eyes burned with the fervor of the true believer above his plaited beard, and his mouth twisted with contempt for those less full of faith than himself. "Many are the voices crying out to witness a sacrifice. Even some who have seen now whisper that the creature sent by the ancient gods has abandoned us, since it has not been seen in so many days. A few, among the newcomers, say that there *is* no sign, that it is all a lie. These last speak now in private places, among themselves, but they will not forever, and I fear the hearts of the doubters may be easily swayed."

Basrakan's teeth ground in frustration. He had had the same fears of abandonment himself, and scourged himself at night, alone, for his lack of belief. He had tried to summon the beast ot fire, tried and failed. But it was still there, he told himself. Still beneath the mountain, waiting to come forth once more. Waiting for—his breath caught in his throat—a sign of their faith.

"How many warriors are gathered?" he demanded.

"More than forty thousand, Imalla, and more come every day. It is a great strain to feed so many, though they are, of course, the faithful."

Basrakan pulled himself to his full height. Renewed belief shone on his dark narrow face. "Let the warriors know that their lack of faith is not secret." He intoned the words, letting them flow from him, convinced they were inspired by the true gods. "Let them know that an act of faith is demanded of them if they would have the sight they crave. A bird will come, a raven, a sign from the spirits of the air. Half of those gathered are to follow it, and it will guide them to unbelievers, soldiers of Zamora. These they must slay, letting none escape. Not one. If this is done as it is commanded, the sight of the true gods' favor will be granted to them."

"A bird," Jbeil breathed. "A sign from the spirits of the air. Truly are the ancient gods mighty, and truly is Basraken Imalla mighty in their sight."

Basrakan waved away the compliment with a negligent hand. "I am but a man," he said. "Now, go! See that it is done as I have commanded."

The black-robed man bowed himself from the sorcerer's presence, and Basrakan began to rub at his temples as soon as he was gone. So many pressures on him. They made his head hurt. But there was the girl. Showing her the evil within her, saving her from it, would ease the pain. He would chastise the lust from her. His face shining with the ascetic look of one who suffered for his duty, Basrakan retraced his steps.

Chapter 11

Djinar lay on his belly in the night and studied the hunter's camp, lying still and quiet on the next hill. His dark robes blended with the shadows of his own stony hilltop. Only smouldering beds of ashes remained of the cook fires, leaving the camp in darkness, its tents and carts but dim mounds, save for the soft glow of lamps within a large tent of scarlet. The moon rode high over the jagged peaks to the north, but dense dark clouds let its pale light through only an occasional brief rent. A perfect night for attack. He tugged at the triple braids of his beard. Perhaps the ancient gods *were* with them.

It had certainly seemed so during the days when the trail of the hunting party led north like an arrow aimed at the encampment of Basraken Imalla. Could it be that the Eyes of Fire were drawn in some fashion to the Imalla, that the true gods stirred themselves among men, even through the Zamoran slut? A chill like the trickle of an icy mountain stream ran

147

down Djinar's spine, and the hairs on the back of his neck rose. It seemed to him that the ancient gods walked the earth within sight of his eyes. Rocks grated behind him; Djinar gasped, and almost fouled himself.

Farouz dropped down beside him on the stony ground.

"Sentries?" Djinar asked finally. He was pleased at the steadiness of his voice.

The other man snorted in contempt. "Ten of them, but all more asleep than awake. They will die easily."

"So many? The soldiers set guards in such numbers, but not hunters."

"I tell you, Djinar, they all but snore. Their eyes are closed."

"A score of eyes," Djinar sighed. "All it takes is one pair to be alert. If the camp is awakened, and we must ride uphill at them. . . ."

"Bah! We should have attacked when first we found them, while they were yet on the march. Or do you still fear the Brythunian dogs? They are gone long since."

Djinar did not answer. Only because Sharmal had gone off alone to answer a call of nature had the Brythunians been seen, ghosting along the trail of the hunters from Shadizar. There was no great love lost between Brythunian and Zamoran, it was true, but either would turn aside from slaying the other to wet his blade with the blood of a hillman. Farouz would have placed them between their two enemies—at

least two score of the Brythunians; half again so
many Zamorans—without a thought save how many
he could kill.

"If your . . . caution brings us to failure," Farouz
muttered, "do not think to shield yourself from
Basrakan Imalla's wrath by casting blame on others.
The truth will be known."

Farouz, Djinar decided, would not survive to return to the Imalla's encampment of the faithful. The
old gods themselves would see the justice of it.

Again boots scrabbled on the rocks behind him,
but this time Djinar merely looked over his shoulder.
Sharmal, a slender young man with his wispy beard
worked into many thin braids, squatted near the two
men. "The Brythunian unbelievers ride yet to the
east," the young man said.

"They did not stop at dark?" Djinar demanded,
frowning. He did not like behavior out of the ordinary,
and men did not travel by night without pressing
reason, not in sight of the Kezankians.

"When I turned back at sundown," Sharmal
answered, "they still rode east. I . . . I did not wish to
miss the fighting."

"If there is to be any," Farouz sneered.

Djinar's teeth ground loudly. "Mount your horses,"
he commanded. "Surround the camp and advance
slowly. Strike no blow until I call, unless the alarm
be given. Well, Farouz? You speak eager words. Can
your arm match them?"

With a snarl Farouz leaped to his feet and dashed

down the hill to where their shaggy, mountain-bred horses waited.

Djinar followed with a grim smile and climbed into the high-pommeled saddle. Carefully he walked his mount around the side of the hill, toward the camp atop the next stony rise. The rattle of unshod hooves on rock did not disturb him, not now. He guided his horse upslope. To the core of him he was convinced the Zamorans would not rouse. The ancient gods were with him. He and the others were one with the dark. He could make out a sentry, leaning on his spear, unseeing, unaware of one more shadow that drifted closer. Djinar loosed his tulwar from its scabbard. The true gods might walk the camp before him, but there was another presence as well. Death. He could smell it. Death for many men. Death for Farouz.

Smiling, Djinar dug in his heels; his mount sprang forward. The sentry had time to widen his eyes in shock; then the curved blade with the strength of Djinar's arm and the weight of the charging horse behind it took the man's head from his shoulders. Djinar's cry rent the darkness. "By the will of the true gods, slay them! No quarter!" Screaming hillmen slashed out of the night with thirsty steel.

Conan's eyes slitted open, where he lay wrapped in his cloak and the night beneath the sky. After her behavior he had chosen not to go to Jondra's tent, despite the lamps that remained invitingly lit even now. It had not been thoughts of the silken body that had wakened him, though, but a sound out of place. He could hear the breathing of the sentry nearest him, a breathing too deeply regular for a man alert. The fools would not hear his advice, he thought. They listened, but would not hear. There were other things they did not hear, as well. The sentry's half-snore was overlaid by another sound; stones slid and clicked on the hillside. On *all* sides of the hill.

"Crom!" he muttered. In a continuous motion he threw aside his black cloak, rose to his feet and drew steel. His mouth opened to shout the alarm, and in that instant there was need no longer.

On the heels of the hollow 'thunk' of a blade striking flesh came, "By the will of the true gods, slay them! No quarter!"

Chaos clawed its way out of the dark, hillmen appearing on every side screaming for the blood of unbelievers, hunters scrambling from their tents crying prayers to their gods for another dawn.

The big Cimmerian ran toward the sentry he had listened to. Shocked to wakefulness the hunter tried to lower his long-pointed spear, but a slashing stroke across the face from a tulwar spun him shrieking to the ground.

"Crom!" Conan roared.

The hillman jerked at his reins, spun his shaggy mount above the downed sentry toward the huge man who loomed out of the night. "The true gods will it!" he yelled. Waving his bloody blade above his turban, he booted his shaggy mount into a charge.

For the space of a heartbeat Conan halted, planted

his feet as if preparing to take the charge. Suddenly he sprang forward, ducking under the whistling crescent of steel, his own blade lancing into the hillman's middle. The shock of the blow rocked the Cimmerian to his heels as the hillman seemed to leap backwards over his horse's rump to crash to earth.

Placing his foot on the chest of the corpse, Conan pulled his sword free. Warned by a primitive sense, by a pricking between his shoulderblades, he whirled to find another mounted foe, and a tulwar streaking for his head. But his steel was rising as he turned, its razor edge slicing through the descending wrist. Tulwar and hand flew, and the keening hillman galloped into the night with the fountaining stump of his wrist held high, as if he could thus keep the blood from pouring out of him.

Already two high-wheeled carts were towering bonfires, and flames swiftly ate five of the round tents. Over all hung the din of battle, the clang of steel on steel, the screams of the wounded, the moans of the dying. Another cart burst afire. The burnings cast back the night from struggling pairs of men who danced with sanguine blades among the bodies that littered the hilltop. Of those who lay still, more wore the mail shirts and spiked helms of Zamorans than wore turbans.

All this Conan took in in an instant, but one sight among all the others drew his eyes. Jondra, drawn from her sleeping furs and naked save for a quiver slung over her shoulder, stood before her crimson-walled tent, nocking arrows and firing as calmly as if she shot her bow at straw targets. And where her shafts went hillmen died.

Another had become aware of her, the Cimmerian saw. A hillman at the far end of the camp suddenly gave an ululating cry and kicked his mount into a gallop for the bare-skinned archer.

"Jondra!" Conan shouted, but even as he did he knew she could not hear above the tumult. Nor would all his speed take him to her side in time.

Tossing his sword to his left hand, he flung himself in two bounds back to the sentry who lay with his face a ruined mask staring at the sable sky. Ruthlessly he put a foot on the man's outstretched arm, ripped free the heavy hunting spear from the death-grip that held it. With desperate quickness he straightened, turned and threw, freezing as the spear left his hand. No will or thought was left for motion, for all rode with that thick shaft. The hillman's mount was but two strides from Jondra, his blade heartbeats from her back, but still she neither heard nor turned. And the hillman convulsed as a forearm-long blade transfixed his chest. His horse galloped on, and he slowly toppled backwards, falling like a sack before the woman he meant to slay. Jondra started as the body hit the ground almost at her feet, but for a moment continued to fumble at her empty quiver in search of another arrow. Abruptly she tossed aside her bow and snatched the tulwar from the dead man's hand.

Conan found he could breathe again. He took a step toward her . . . and something sliced a line of fire across his back. The big youth threw himself into a forward roll and came to his feet searching for his attacker. There were men behind him, both hillmen and hunters, but all save Arvaneus and Telades were killing or being killed, and even as he looked they engaged turbanned foes. He had no time to seek out particular enemies, Conan thought. There were enough for all. The dark blood-rage rose in him, cold enough to burn.

When he turned back Jondra was gone, but thoughts of her were buried deep now in the battle-black of his mind. Some men are said to be born for battle; Conan had been born on the field of battle. The scent drawn in with his first breath had been the coppery smell of fresh-spilled blood. The first sound to greet his ears had been the clash of steel. The first sight his eye beheld had been ravens circling in the sky, waiting till living men departed and they ruled what remained.

With the battle fury that had been his birthright he strode through the flames and screams of the encampment, and death rode on his steel. He sought the turbanned men, the bearded men, and those he found went before Erlik's Black Throne with eyes of azure fire their last memory of the world of men. His ancient broadsword flashed banefully in the light of burning tents, flashed till its encrimsoned length could flash no more, but seemed rather to eat light as it ate life. Men faced him, men fell before him, and at last men fled him.

The time came when he stood alone, and no turbans could his questing eye find but those on dead men. There were standing men, he realized as the haze of battle-rage thinned and cleared his eyes, Zamoran hunters gathered in a loose circle about him, staring in wonder tinged with fear. He turned to face each man in turn, and each fell back a step at his gaze. Even Arvaneus could not hold his ground, though his face flushed with anger when he realized what he had done.

"The hillmen?" Conan demanded hoarsely. He stripped the rough woolen cloak from a hillman's corpse and wiped his blade clean.

"Gone," Telades said in a high voice. He paused to clear his throat. "Some few fled, I think, but most. . . ." His gesture took in the entire hilltop, strewn with bodies and burned-out tents, illumined by flaming carts. "It was your work that saved us, Cimmerian."

"Hannuman's Stones!" Arvaneus roared. "Are you all women? It was your own arms saved you, swords in your own hands! If the barbar slew one or two, it was his skin he sought to save."

"Do not speak the fool," Telades retorted. "You of all men should not speak against him. Conan fought like a demon while the rest of us struggled to realize that we were awake, that it was not a nightmare we faced." A murmur of agreement came from the circle of men.

Face twisted darkly, Arvaneus opened his mouth, but Conan cut him off. "If some of them escaped, they may return with others. We should be gone from this place, and quickly.''

"There stands your hero," Arvaneus sneered. "Ready to run. Few hillman bands are larger than the number which attacked us, and most of them now wait for the worms. Who else will come against us? I, for one, think we slew all of the mountain dogs.''

"Some did flee," Telades protested, but Arvaneus spoke on over him.

"I saw none escaping. If I had, they wouldn't have lived to escape. If we run like rabbits, then like rabbits we run from shadows.''

"Your insults begin to disturb me, huntsman," Conan said, hefting his sword. "In the past I have forborne killing you for one reason or another. Now, it is time for you to still your tongue, or I will still it for you.''

Arvaneus stared stiffly back at him, his tulwar twitching in his hand, but he did not speak. The other hunters moved back to give room.

Into the silence Jondra stepped, a robe of brocaded sky-blue silk covering her to the ankles and held tightly at her neck with both hands. She studied the two men confronting each other before speaking. "Conan, why do you think the hillmen will return?''

She was attempting to ignore the tension, the Cimmerian knew, and so disarm it, but he thought the answer to her question was more important than killing Arvaneus. "It is true that bands of hillmen are ususally small, but in Shadizar it is said the Kezankian tribes are gathering. The soldiers we saw marching north bear this out, for it is also said the army is being sent to deal with them. To go risks nothing; to stay risks that the few who fled may bring back a thousand more.''

''A thousand!'' the hawk-faced man snorted. ''My lady, it is well known how the hill tribes war constantly with one another. A thousand hillmen in one place would kill each other in the space of a day. And if, by some miracle, so many were gathered together, their attention would surely be on the soldiers. In any case, I cannot believe in this bazaar rumor of a gathering of the tribes. It goes against all that I know of the hillmen.''

Jondra nodded thoughtfully, then asked, ''And our injured? How many are they, and how badly hurt?''

''Many nicks and cuts, my lady,'' Arvaneus told her, ''but only fourteen hurt badly enough to be accounted as wounded, and but two of those seriously.'' He hesitated. ''Eleven are dead, my lady.''

''Eleven,'' she sighed, and her eyes closed.

'' 'Twould have been more, my lady, save for Conan,'' Telades said, and Arvaneus rounded on him.

''Cease your chatter of the barbar, man!''

''Enough!'' Jondra barked. Her voice stilled the hunters on the instant. ''I will reach a decision on what is to be done tomorrow. For now the wounded must be tended, and the fires put out. Arvaneus, you will see to it.'' She paused to take a deep breath, looking at no one. ''Conan, come to my tent. Please?'' The last word was forced, and as she said it she turned away quickly, her robe flaring to give a glimpse of bare thighs, and hurried from the circle of men.

Conan's visits to Jondra's tent and sleeping furs had been an open secret, but an unacknowledged one. Studiously the men all avoided looking at Conan, or at each other, for that matter. Arvaneus seemed stunned. Tamira alone met his eyes, and she glared daggers.

With a shake of his head for the vagaries of women, the big Cimmerian sheathed his sword and followed Jondra.

She was waiting for him in her scarlet tent. As he ducked through the tent-flap, she slipped the silk robe from her shoulders, and he found his arms full of sleek bare skin. Full breasts bored into his ribs as she clutched at him, burying her head against his broad chest.

"I . . . I should not have spoken as I did earlier," she murmured. "I do not doubt what you saw, and I do not want you to stay away from my bed."

"It is well you believe me," he said, smoothing her hair, "for I saw as I said. But now is no time to speak of that." She sighed and snuggled closer, if that was possible. "It is time to speak of turning back. Your hunters have taken grievous hurt from the hillmen, and you are yet a day from the mountains. Do you enter the mountains with carts and oxen, you'll not escape further attention from the tribes. Your men will be slain, and you will find yourself the slave of an unwashed tribesman whose wives will beat you constantly for your beauty. At least, they will until the harsh life and the labor leaches your youth as it does theirs.''

Word by word she had stiffened in his arms. Now she pushed herself from him, staring up at him incredulously. "It has been long years," she said in breathless fury, "since I apologized to any man, and never have I b . . . asked one to my bed before you. Whatever I expected for doing so, it was not to be lectured.''

"It must be spoken of." He found it hard to ignore the heavy, round breasts that confronted him, the tiny waist that flared into generous hips and long legs, but he forced himself to speak as if she were draped in layers of thick wool. "The hillmen are roused. Ants might escape their notice, but not men. And should you find this beast you hunt, remember that it is a hunter as well, and one that kills with fire. How many men will you see roasted alive to put a trophy on your wall?''

"A folk tale," she scoffed. "If hillmen cannot frighten me off, do you think I will run before a myth?''

"Eldran," he began with a patience he no longer felt, but her screach cut him off.

"No! I will not hear of that . . . that Brythunian!'' Panting, she struggled to gain control of herself. At last she drew herself up imperiously. "I did not summon you here for argument. You will come to my bed and speak only of what we do, or you will leave me.''

Conan's anger coiled to within a hair's breadth of

erupting, but he managed to keep his reply to a mocking, "As my lady wishes." And he turned his back on her nudity.

Her furious cries followed him into the fading night, echoing across the camp. "Conan! Come back here, Mitra blast you! You cannot leave me like this! I command you to return, Erlik curse you forever!"

No man looked up from his labor, but it was clear from the intensity with which they minded their work that none was deaf. Those prodding burning bundles from the carts with spears abruptly redoubled their efforts to save what had not already caught fire. The newly set sentries suddenly peered at the failing shadows as if each hid a hillman.

Tamira was passing among the wounded, lying in a row on blankets in the middle of the camp, holding a waterskin to each man's mouth. She looked up with a bright smile as he passed. "So you'll sleep alone again tonight, Cimmerian," she said sweetly. "A pity." Conan did not look at her, but a scowl darkened his face.

One of the carts had been abandoned to burn, and flaming bundles lay scattered about the others. The fat cook capered among the men, waving a pewter tray over his head and complaining loudly at their use of his implements for shoveling dirt onto the fires. Conan took the tray from the rotund man's hands and bent beside Telades to dig at the rocky soil.

The shaven-headed hunter eyed him sideways for a time, then said carefully, "There are few men would walk out on her without reason."

Instead of answering the unasked question, Conan snarled, "I've half a mind to tie her to her horse so you can lead her back to Shadizar."

"You've half a mind if you think that you could," Telades said, throwing a potful of dirt and small stones on a fiery bale, "or that we would. The Lady Jondra decides where to go, and we follow."

"Into the Kezankians?" Conan said incredulously. "With the tribes stirring? The army didn't come north for the weather."

"I've served the House Perashanid," the other man said slowly, "since I was a boy, and my father before me, and his before him. The Lady Jondra *is* the house, now, for she is the last. I cannot desert her. But you could, I suppose. In fact, perhaps you should."

"And why would I do that?" Conan asked drily.

Telades answered as though the question had been serious. "Not all spears are thrown by the enemies you expect, northlander. If you do stay, watch your back."

Conan paused in the act of stooping for more dirt. So the spear that grazed his back had not been cast by a hillman's hand. Arvaneus, no doubt. Or perhaps some other, long in the Perashanid's service, who did not like the last daughter of the house bedding a landless warrior. That was all he needed. An enemy behind him—at least one—and the hillmen surrounding. Tomorrow, he decided, he would make one last try at convincing Jondra to turn back. And Tamira, as well. There were gems aplenty in Shadizar for her to steal. And if they would not, he would leave them and go back alone. Furiously he scooped dirt onto the tray and hurled it at the flames. He would! Erlik take him if he did not.

In the gray dawn Djinar stared at the pitiful following that remained to him. Five men with shocked eyes and no horses.

"It was the giant," Sharmal muttered. His turban was gone, and his face was streaked with dirt, and dried blood from a scalp wound. His eye focused on something none of the rest could see. "The giant slew who he would. None could face him." No one tried to quiet him, for the mad were touched by the old gods, and under their protection.

"Does any man think we can yet take the Eyes of Fire from the Zamoran woman?" Djinar asked tiredly. Blank stares answered him.

"He cut off Farouz's hand," Sharmal said. "The blood spurted from Farouz's arm as he rode into the night to die."

Djinar ignored the youth. "And does any man doubt the price we will pay for failing Basrakan Imalla's command?" Again the four who retained their senses kept silent, but again the answer was in their dark eyes, colored now by a tinge of horror.

Sharmal began to weep. "The giant was a spirit of the earth. We have displeased the true gods, and they sent him to punish us."

"It is decided, then." Djinar shook his head. He would leave much behind, including his favorite saddle and two young wives, but such could be more easily replaced than blood from a man's veins. "In the south the tribes have not yet heeded Basrakan's call. They care only for raiding the caravans to Sultanapur and Aghrapur. We will go there. Better the risk no one will take us in than the certainty of Basrakan's anger."

He did not see Sharmal move, but suddenly the young man's fist thudded against his chest. He looked down, perplexed that his breath seemed short. The blow had not been that hard. Then he saw the hilt of a dagger in the fist. When he raised his eyes again, the other four were gone, unwilling to meddle in the affairs of a madman.

"You have been attainted, Djinar," Sharmal said in a tone suitable for instructing a child. "Better this than that you should flee the will of the true gods. Surely you see that. We must return to Basrakan Imalla, who is a holy man, and tell him of the giant."

He had been right, Djinar thought. Death had been in that camp. He could smell it still. He opened his mouth to laugh, and blood poured out.

Chapter 12

Amid the lengthening shadows of mid-afternoon, some semblance of normality had returned to the hunter's camp. The fires were out, and those carts that could not be salvaged had been pushed to the bottom of the hill, along with supplies too badly burned for use. Most of the wounded were on their feet, if not ready for another battle, and the rest soon would be. The dead—including now the two most seriously wounded—had been buried in a row on the hillside, with cairns of stones laid atop their graves to keep the wolves from them. Zamoran dead, at least, had been treated so. Vultures and ravens squawked and contended beyond the next hill, where the corpses of hillmen had been dragged.

Sentries were set now not only about the hilltop camp itself, but on the hills surrounding. Those distant watchers, mounted so they could bring an alarm in time to be useful, had been Conan's idea. When he put the notion forward Jondra ignored it, and

165

Arvaneus scorned it, but the sentries were placed, if without acknowledgement to the Cimmerian.

It was not for pique, however, that Conan stalked through the camp with a face like a thunderhead. He cared nothing who got credit for the sentries, so long as they were placed. But all day Jondra had avoided him. She had hurried about checking the wounded, checking the meals the cook prepared, meddling in a score of tasks she would normally have dismissed once she ordered them done. All in the camp save Conan she had kept at the run. And every particle of it, he knew, was to keep from talk with him.

Tamira trotted by in her short white tunic, intently balancing a flagon of wine and a goblet on a tray, and Conan caught her arm. "I can't stop now," she said distractedly. "She wants this right away, and the way she's been today I have no wish to be slow." Suddenly the slender thief chuckled. "Perhaps it would have been better for us all if you *hadn't* slept alone last night."

"Never mind that," Conan growled. "It's time for leaving, Tamira. Tomorrow will see us in the mountains."

"Is that what you said to Jondra to anger her so?" Her face tightened. "Did you ask her to go back with you, too?"

"Fool girl, will you listen? A hunting trophy is no reason to risk death at the hands of hillmen, nor are those gems."

"What of Jondra?" she said suspiciously. "She won't turn back."

"If I can't talk her into it, I will go without her. Will you come?"

Tamira bit her full under-lip and studied his face from beneath her lashes. Finally, she nodded. "I will. It must be in the night, though, while she sleeps. She'll not let me leave her service, if she knows of it. What would she do without a handmaiden to shout at? But what of your own interest in the rubies, Cimmerian?"

"I no longer have any interest," he replied.

"No longer have," Tamira began, then broke off with a disbelieving shake of her head. "Oh, you must think I am a fine fool to believe that, Cimmerian. Or else you're one. Mitra, but I do keep forgetting that men will act like men."

"And what does that mean?" Conan demanded.

"That she's had you to her bed, and now you will not steal from her. And you call yourself a thief!"

"My reasons are no concerns of yours," he told her with more patience than he felt. "No more than the rubies should be. You leave with me tonight, remember?"

"I remember," she said slowly. As her large brown eyes looked up at him, he thought for a moment that she wanted to say something more.

"Lyana!" Jondra's voice cracked in the air like a whip. "Where is my wine?"

"Whcre is my wine?" Tamira muttered mockingly, but she broke into a run, dodging around Telades, who labored under one end of a weighty brass-bound chest.

"Mayhap you shouldn't have angered her, Cimmerian," the shaven-headed hunter panted. "Mayhap you could apologize." The man at the other end of the chest nodded weary agreement.

"Crom!" Conan growled. "Is everyone in the camp worrying about whether I. . . ." His words trailed off as one of the sentries galloped his horse up the hill. Unknowingly, easing his broadsword in its scabbard, he strode to where the man was dismounting before Jondra. The hunters left off their tasks to gather around.

"Soldiers, my lady," the sentry said, breathing heavily. "Cavalry. Two, perhaps three hundred of them, coming hard."

Jondra pounded a fist on a rounded thigh. Her salmon silk tunic and riding breeches were dusty and sweat-stained from her day's labors. "Erlik take all soldiers," she said tightly, then took a deep breath that made her heavy breasts stir beneath the taut silk of her tunic. "Very well. If they come, I'll receive their commander. Arvaneus! See that any man who's bandaged is out of sight. If the soldiers arrive before I return, be courteous, but tell them nothing. Nothing, understand me! Lyana! Attend me, girl!" Before she finished speaking she was pushing through the assembled hunters, not waiting for them to move from her path.

The hawk-faced huntsman began shouting commands, and hunters and carters scattered in all directions, hastening to prepare the camp for visitors. Moving the wounded inside tents was the least of it, for most of them could walk without assistance, but Jondra's industriousness had left bales and bundles, piles of cooking gear and stacks of spears scattered among the remaining tents till the camp seemed struck by a whirlwind.

Ignoring the bustle behind him, Conan settled into a flat-footed crouch at the edge of the camp, his eyes intent on the direction from which the sentry had come. More than once his hand strayed unconsciously to the worn hilt of his ancient broadsword. He did not doubt that the sentry had seen Zamoran soldiers and not hillmen, but he had as little regard for one as for the other. Relations between the army and a thief were seldom easy.

A ringing clatter of shod hooves on loose stone heralded the soldiers' approach well before the mounted column came into sight. In ranks of four, with well-aligned lance-points glittering in the afternoon sun, they wended their way along the small valleys between the hills. A banner led them, such as Zamoran generals were wont to have, of green silk fringed with gold, its surface embroidered in ornate gold script recounting victories. Conan snorted contemptuously at the sight of the honor standard. At that distance he could not read the script, but he could count the number of battles listed. Considering the number of true battles fought by Zamoran arms in the twenty years past, that banner gave honor to many a border skirmish and brawl with brigands.

At the foot of the hill the column drew up, two files wheeling to face the camp, the other two turning their mounts the other way. The standard bearer and the general, marked by the plume of scarlet horsehair on his golden helmet and the gilding of his mail, picked their way up the hill through the few stunted trees and scattered clumps of waist-high scrub.

At Arvaneus' impatient signal two of the hunters ran forward, one to hold the general's bridle, the other his stirrup, as he dismounted. He was a tall man of darkly handsome face, his upper lip adorned by thin mustaches. His arrogant eye ran over the camp, pausing at Conan for a raised brow of surprise and a sniff of dismissal before going on. The Cimmerian wondered idly if the man had ever actually had to use the jewel-hilted sword at his side.

"Well," the general said suddenly, "where is your mistress?"

Arvaneus darted forward, his face set for effusive apologies, but Jondra's voice brought him to a skidding halt. "Here I am, Zathanides. And what does Zamora's most illustrious general do so far from the palaces of Shadizar?"

She came before the general with a feline stride, and her garb brought gasps even from her hunters. Shimmering scarlet silk, belted with thickly woven gold and pearls, moulded every curve of breasts and belly and thighs, rounded and firm enough to make a eunuch's mouth water.

It was not the raiment that drew Conan's attention, however. On her head rested a diadem of sapphires and black opals, with one great ruby larger than the last joint of a big man's thumb lying above her brows. Between her generous breasts nestled that ruby's twin, depending from a necklace likewise encrusted with brilliant azure sapphires and opals of deepest ebon. The Cimmerian's gaze sought out Tamira. The young woman thief was demurely presenting to Zathanides a tray bearing a golden goblet and a crystal flagon of wine, with damp, folded cloths beside. She seemed unaware of the gems she had meant to steal.

"You are as lovely as ever, Jondra," the general said as he wiped his hands and tossed the cloths back onto the tray. "But that loveliness might have ended gracing some hillman's hut if I hadn't found this fellow Eldran."

Jondra stiffened visibly. "Eldran?"

"Yes. A Brythunian. Hunter, he said." He took the goblet Tamira filled for him, gracing her with a momentary smile that touched only his lips. "I wouldn't have believed his tale of a Zamoran noblewoman in this Mitra-forsaken place if it had not been for his description. A woman as tall as most men, ravingly beautiful of face and figure, a fair shot with a bow. And your gray eyes, of course. I knew then it could be none but you." He tilted back his head to drink.

"He dared describe me so? A fair shot?" She hissed the words, but it had been "ravingly beautiful" that made her face color, and the mention of her eyes that had clenched her fists. "I hope you have this Eldran well chained. And his followers. I . . . I have reason to believe they are brigands."

Conan grinned openly. She was not a woman to take kindly to being bested.

"I fear not," Zathanides said, tossing the empty goblet back to Tamira. "He seemed what he called himself, and he was alone, so I sent him on his way. In any case, you should be thankful to him for saving your life, Jondra. The hillmen are giving trouble, and this is no place for one of your little jaunts. I'll send a few men with you to see that you get back to Shadizar safely."

"I am no child to be commanded," Jondra said hotly.

The general's heavy-lidded eyes caressed her form, and his reply came slowly. "You are certainly no child, Jondra. No, indeed. But go you must."

Jondra's eyes flickered to Conan. Abruptly her posture softened, and her voice became languorous. "No, I am not a child, Zathanides. Perhaps we can discuss my future plans. In the privacy of my tent?"

Startlement passed over Zathanides' face to be replaced by pleasure. "Certainly," he said with an unctuous smile. "Let us . . . discuss your future."

Arvaneus' swarthy face was a blend of despair and rage as he watched the pair disappear into the scarlet tent. Conan merely scooped up a handful of rocks and began tossing them down the hill one by one. Telades squatted next to him.

"More trouble, Cimmerian," the shaven-headed man said, "and I begin to wonder if you are worth it."

"What have I to do with anything?" Conan asked coldly.

"She does this because of you, you fool north-lander."

"She makes her choice." He would not admit even to himself that this flirting with Zathanides sat ill with him. "She's not the first woman to choose a man for wealth and titles."

"But she is no ordinary woman. I have served her since she was a child, and I tell you that you were the first man to come to her bed."

"I know," Conan said through gritted teeth. He was unused to women casting him aside; he liked neither the fact of it nor the discussing of it.

A woman's scream came from the tent, and the Cimmerian threw another stone. The tightness of his jaw eased, and a slight smile touched his lips. Arvaneus took a single step toward the scarlet pavilion, then froze in indecision. From where she knelt by the tent flap, Tamira cast an agonized glance at Conan. All the rest of the camp seemed stunned to immobility. Another shriek rent the air.

Telades leaped to his feet, but Conan caught the hunter's arm. "I will see if she requires aid," he said calmly, tossing aside his handful of stones. Despite his tone the Cimmerian's first steps were quick, and by the time he reached the tent he was running.

As he ducked through the tent-flap, the story was plain. Jondra struggled among the cushions, her scarlet robe rucked up above her rounded hips, long legs kicking in the air, while Zathanides lay half atop her, fumbling with his breeches and raining kisses on her face. Her small fists pounded futilely at his back and sides.

With a snarl Conan grasped the man by the neck of his gilded mail shirt and the seat of his breeches, lifting him straight into the air. Zathanides gave a shout, then began cursing and struggling, clawing at his sword, but the huge Cimmerian easily carried him to the entrance and threw him from the tent to land like a sack.

Conan took a bare instant to assure himself that Jondra was unharmed. Her jewelry was discarded on the cushions, and her robe was torn to expose one smooth shoulder, but she seemed more angry than hurt as she scrambled to her feet, pushing her silk down over her sleek nudity. Then he followed Zathanides outside. The general had risen to one knee, his mouth twisted with rage, and his sword came out as Conan appeared. The Cimmerian's foot lashed out. The jeweled sword went flying; Zathanides yelped and clutched his wrist. The shout of outraged pain faded as Conan's blade point touched the general's throat.

"Stop!" Jondra cried. "Conan, put up your sword!"

Conan lowered his steel slowly, though he did not sheath it. It had been she who was assaulted, and by his thinking Zathanides' life was hers to dispose of as she saw fit, or even to spare. But he would not disarm himself until the man was dead or gone.

"I'll have your head, barbarian," Zathanides snarled

as he got painfully to his feet. "You'll discover the penalty for attacking a Lord of Zamora."

"Then you will discover the penalty for . . . for manhandling a Lady of Zamora," Jondra said coldly. "Tread warily, Zathanides, for your head and Conan's will share the same fate, and the choice is yours."

Zathanides' dark eyes bulged, and spittle dripped from the corner of his mouth. "Make what charges you will, you half-breed Brythunian trull. Do you think there is anyone in Zamora who has not heard the stories of you? That you bed a man before you take him in service as a hunter? Who will believe that one such as I would touch such a slut, such a piece of—"

He cut off and took a step back as Conan's sword lifted again, but Jondra grabbed the Cimmerian's massive arm, though both her hands could not come near encircling it. "Hold, Conan," she said unsteadily. "Make your choice, Zathanides."

The dark-faced general scrubbed at the spittle on his chin with the back of his hand, then nodded jerkily. " 'Tis you who has made a choice, Jondra. Keep your savage lover. Enter the mountains if you will, and find a hillman." Stamping to where his jewel-hilted blade lay, he snatched it from the ground and slammed it home in the sheath at his side. "For all I care, you can go straight to Zandru's Ninth Hell!"

Satisfaction glimmered beneath Conan's anger as he watched the general's stiff-backed march to his horse. Zathanides might wish to abandon Jondra to her fate, but too many of his own soldiers knew that he had found her. The attempted rape might well be covered up—especially if other nobles felt about Jondra as the general did—but failing in his attempt to turn a woman back from the mountains would place his manhood in an unfavorable light indeed. At least, that was the way the Cimmerian believed a man of Zathanides' ilk would look at the matter. Conan felt he could safely wager that the next day would see the appearance of a force under orders to escort the hunting party to Shadizar, without regard for what Jondra had to say.

As Zathanides and his standard bearer galloped down the hill, Arvaneus approached the crimson-walled tent, his manner at once arrogant and hesitant. "My lady," he said hoarsely, "if you command it, I will take men and see that Lord Zathanides does not survive the night."

"If I command it," Jondra replied in an icy tone, "you will sneak in the night and murder Zathanides. Conan did not await my command. He faced Zathanides openly, without fear of consequences."

"My lady, I . . . I would die for you. I live only for you."

Jondra turned her back on the impassioned huntsman. Her eyes fastened on Conan's broad chest as if afraid to meet his gaze. "You begin to make a habit of saving me," she said softly. "I see no reason for us to continue to sleep apart." Arvaneus's teeth ground audibly.

Conan said nothing. If his thoughts concerning

Zathanides were correct, then he should be gone from the camp before the night ended, for the general's instructions would certainly include the death of one large northlander. Too, there was his plan of departing with Tamira. Leaving from Jondra's bed would necessitate explanations he did not want to make.

The tall noblewoman drew a shuddering breath. "I am no tavern wench to be toyed with. I will have an answer now."

"I did not leave your bed for wanting to," he said carefully, and cursed his lack of diplomatic skill when her chin went up and her eyes flared. "Let us not argue," he added quickly. "It will be days before the wounded have their strength back. They should be days of rest and enjoyment." Days spent in her return to Shadizar, he thought, but his satisfaction vanished at her scornful laugh.

"Can you be so foolish? Zathanides will brood on his manhood and the pride he lost here, then convince himself that he can escape any charges I might bring. Tomorrow will see more soldiers, Conan, no doubt with orders to take me back in chains if I'll go no other way. But they will need to seek me in the mountains." Abruptly her face stilled, and her voice hardened. "You are *not* so foolish as that. You know as well as I the soldiers will return. You would have waited and seen me carried back to Shadizar like a bundle. Well, go, if you fear the mountains. Go! I care not!" As abruptly as she had turned her back on Arvaneus, she turned to face the huntsman again. "I intend to press on at first light," she told the hawk-

faced man, "and to move quickly. All baggage must
be discarded except what can be carried on pack
animals. The wounded and all men who cannot be
mounted will turn back with the ox-carts. Perhaps
their trail will confuse Zathanides for a time. . . ."

As her list of instructions went on, Arvaneus shot
a look over her shoulder at Conan, smug satisfaction
mingled with a promise of violence. There would be
more trouble from that quarter. Or rather, the Cimmerian reminded himself, there would be if he continued with the hunters, which he had no intention of
doing. And since such was his plan, it was time for
him to be making preparations for his leave-taking.

Slowly Conan moved away from the noblewoman's
flow of commands. With studied casualness he drifted
beyond the cookfires. The fat cook, frowning over a
delicate dish for Jondra's table, never looked up as
the Cimmerian rooted among the supplies. When
Conan walked on, he carried two fat leather pouches
of dried meat in the crook of his arm. Taking one
quick look to make certain he was unobserved, he
cached the meat beneath a thornbush on the edge of
the encampment. Soon he had added four waterbags,
and blankets of blue-striped wool. He was inured to
sleeping with naught but his cloak for protection
from the cold, or even without it, but he could not
think a city woman like Tamira was so hardy.

The horses had to wait until the point of leaving—
they certainly could not be saddled now without drawing unwanted attention—but he walked to the picket
line anyway. It was easier to choose out a good

mount when there was light to see. The big black he
had been riding would do for him; Tamira needed a
horse with good endurance as well, though. He had
intended to move down the line of animals without
stopping, so as to give no hint of his interest, but as
he came to a long-legged bay mare—just the sort he
would choose for Tamira—his feet halted of their
own accord. On the ground at the mare's head rested
a high-pommeled saddle, a bulging waterbag, and a
tightly tied leather sack.

"In the night, Tamira?" he said softly. "Or while
I sit waiting for darkness to come?" The picture of
the rubies lying on the cushions of Jondra's tent was
suddenly bright in his mind.

With a calm he did not feel, Conan strode through
the camp, his eyes seeking Tamira. Once more the
encampment was an anthill, hunters scurrying at
Jondra's commands. For an instant the noblewoman
paused, gazing at Conan as if she wished to speak, or
waited for him to speak, but when he did not slow
she turned angrily back to supervising the preparations for the next morning. Nowhere did Conan see
Tamira. But that, he thought grimly, might mean he
was not too late.

Conan knew how he would have entered the scarlet tent, had he chosen to steal the rubies with the
camp aroused. A glance told him no one was watching,
and he quickly slipped behind Jondra's pavilion. Down
the back of the tent a long slit had been made. Parting
it a fingerwidth, he peered in. Tamira knelt within,
rooting among the cushions. With a muffled laugh

she drew out the sparkling length of the necklace. The tiara was gripped in her other hand.

Soundlessly Conan slipped through the slit. The first announcement of his presence Tamira received was his hand closing over her mouth. His free arm encircled her, pinning her arms and lifting her before she had time to do more than gasp into his palm. She had dropped the gems, he saw, but that was the end of his moment of peace. Tamira exploded into a wriggling, kicking, biting bundle. And footsteps were approaching the front of the tent.

With a muttered oath the Cimmerian ducked back through the slit with his struggling burden. Behind the tent was no place to stop, however, not if someone was going to enter the tent, not with Tamira as likely as not to scream that *he* had been thieving. Cursing under his breath, he scrambled down the stony slope until he found a clump of scrub brush that hid them from the camp. There he tried to set her down, but she kicked him fiercely on the ankle, rocks slid beneath his foot, and he found himself on the ground with Tamira beneath him, her eyes starting from her head from the force of the fall.

"You great oaf!" she wheezed after a moment. "Do you try to break my ribs?"

"I did not kick myself," he growled. "I thought we agreed to leave in the night. What were you doing in Jondra's tent?"

"Nothing was said about the rubies," she retorted. "I haven't changed my plans for them, even if you have. Perhaps," she finished angrily, "you find what

Jondra gives you more valuable than rubies, but as I am not a man I have a different view of the matter.''

"Leave Jondra out of this," he snapped. "And do not try to change the subject. You have a horse waiting this very instant."

Tamira shifted uneasily beneath him, and her eyes slid away from his. "I wanted to be ready," she muttered. "For the night."

"Do you think I'm a fool," he said, "that I take you for a fool? The saddle cannot escape discovery till nightfall. But if someone planned to steal the rubies and leave the camp within the turn of a glass. . . . You could not have been planning such a thing, could you?"

"They would not have held you to blame." Her tone was sullenly excusatory. "Jondra would not blame you if she found you with the rubies in your pouch. And if she did, it would be less than you deserve."

"Jondra," he breathed. "Always Jondra. What is it to you whose bed I share? You and I are not lovers."

Tamira's large brown eyes grew even wider. Scarlet suffused her cheeks, and her mouth worked for a long moment before sound finally came out. "We most certainly are not!" she gasped. "How dare you suggest such a thing? Let me up! Get off me, you great ox! Let me up, I say!" Her small fists punctuated her words, pounding at his shoulders, but suddenly her fingers had tangled in his hair, and she was pressing her lips to his.

Conan blinked once in surprise, then returned her kiss with as much fervor as she was putting into it. "Don't think this will convince me to stay," he said when they broke apart for air. "I'm not such a fool."

"If you stop," she moaned, "then you *are* a fool."

With one last silent reminder that he would *not* be a fool, Conan gave up talk and thought alike for pleasures at once simpler and more complex.

Chapter 13

He was not a fool, Conan told himself once more as he guided his horse along a trail halfway up a nameless peak on the fringe of the Kezankians. If he kept saying it, he thought he might convince himself in time. Before and behind him stretched the hunting party, all mounted and many leading pack animals, wending their way deeper into the hillman domains. The sun stood barely above the horizon. They had left the camp in the hills before the first glimmer of dawn. The ox-carts with the wounded would be on their way back to Shadizar.

Lost in his own thoughts, Conan was surprised to find that Jondra had reined aside to await him. He had not spoken to her since she turned her back on him, but he noted that at least she was smiling now.

She drew her horse in beside his. The trail was wide enough for the animals to walk abreast. "The day is fine, is it not?" she said brightly.

Conan merely looked at her.

"I hoped you would come to me in the night. No, I promised myself I would not say that." Shyly she peered at him through lowered lashes. "I knew you could not leave me. That is . . . I thought . . . you *did* stay because of me, did you not?"

"I did," he said glumly, but she appeared not to notice his tone.

"I knew it," she said, her smile even more radiant than before. "Tonight we will put the past behind us once and for all." With that she galloped up the line of mounted men to resume her place at their head.

Conan growled deep in his throat.

"What did she want?" Tamira demanded, guiding her mount up beside his. It was the same bay mare she had chosen out for her flight. She glared jealously after the noblewoman.

"Nothing of consequence," Conan replied.

The young woman thief grunted contemptuously. " 'Tis likely she thinks you are still here because of the over-generous charms she displays so freely. But you came because of me. Didn't you?"

"I came for you," Conan told her. "But unless you want to see how strongly Jondra wields a switch, you had best not let her see us talking too often."

"Let her but try."

"Then you intend to explain to her that you are not Lyana the handmaiden, but Tamira the thief?"

"If she faced me in a fair fight," the slender woman began with a toss of her head, then broke off in a laugh. "But it is not talk I want from you. She can have that. Till tonight, Conan."

The big Cimmerian sighed heavily as she let her horse fall behind his. It was no easy task he had ahead of him, and all because he could not allow a woman who had shared his bed—much less two of them—to enter the Kezankians while he rode back to Shadizar. He supposed those men who called themselves civilized and him barbarian could have managed it easily. It was beyond him, though, and his pride was enough to make him believe he could bring both safely out of the mountains. Of course, he knew, soon or late each woman would find out about the other. At that point, he was sure, he would rather face all the hillmen of the Kezankians than those two females.

The thought of hillmen brought him back to his surroundings. If he did not keep watch, they might not even make it fully into the mountains, much less out. His eyes scanned the steep brown mountain slopes around him, dotted with tress bizarrely sculpted by wind and harsh clime. He searched the jagged peaks ahead. No signs of life did he discern, but the breeze brought a sound to him, faint yet disturbing. It came from behind.

He reined his horse around to look back, and felt the hair stir on the back of his neck. Far below and far distant among the foothills a battle raged. He could make out little save dust rising as smoke from the hills and the small forms of men swarming like ants, yet for an instant he saw what he could swear was a Zamoran honor standard atop a hill. Then it was ridden down, and the men who rode over it wore

turbans. Most of the other shapes he could make out
were turbanned as well.

"What is the matter?" Jondra shouted, galloping
down the trail. She had to force her way through a
knot of hunters gathered behind Conan. "Why are
you halted?"

" 'Tis a battle, my lady," Telades said, shading
his eyes with one hand to peer down at the hills. "I
cannot say who fights."

"Hillmen," Conan said. "From the look of it
hillmen are killing some part of the Zamoran army."

"Nonsense!" Arvaneus snapped. "The army would
sweep any hillman rabble aside. Besides, the tribes
never gather in such numbers, and . . . and. . . ."
The force of his words weakened as he spoke, and he
finished lamely with, "It is impossible to make out
details at this distance. That could be anyone fighting.
Perhaps it is not a battle at all."

"Perhaps it is a folk dance," Conan said dryly.

Jondra touched his arm. "Is there aught we can do
to aid them?"

"Not even if we had wings," the big Cimmerian
replied.

Relief was writ plain on the faces of the hunters at
his reply, but it was relief tinged with fear. It was all
very well to talk of entering the Kezankians and
risking the wrath of the hill tribes. To actually see
that wrath, even at a distance, was something else,
and most especially when it seemed to be dealt out
by more hillmen than a man might expect to see in a
lifetime of roaming the mountains.

Jondra looked from face to face, then put on a smile. "If so many hillmen are down there, then we shall have the mountains to ourselves." Her words had little effect on the hunters' expressions. A raven appeared, flying around the side of the mountain. "There," Jondra said, drawing her bow from its lacquered case behind her saddle. "Should there be a hillman or two left in the mountains, we'll deal with them as easily as this." Her bowstring slapped against her forearm leather; the raven's wings folded, and the bird dropped like a stone. Conan thought he heard her mutter something about "Brythunian" as she recased her bow. "Now let us ride," she commanded, and galloped back up the trail.

Slowly the column of hunters formed again behind the noblewoman. As Tamira passed Conan, she gave him an anxious, wide-eyed look. Perhaps he *was* a fool, he thought, but he could be no other than what he was. With a reassuring smile for the young woman thief, he joined the file of horsemen picking its way up the mountain.

Eldran ran a judicious eye over the two score men following him through a field of boulders deeper into the mountains, and said, "We stop for a rest."

"About time," said a round-cheeked man with gray streaking the long hair that was held back from his face by a leather cord. "We've ridden since before first light, and I'm not so young as I once was."

"If you tell me about your old bones one more time, Haral," Eldran laughed, and the others joined in, though their laughter was strained. Haral's age and plumpness were belied by the scars on his face, and the wolf whose fur trimmed his cloak had been slain with his bare hands. "A short stop only," Eldran went on. "These mountains feel ill, and I would be done with what we came for and out of them quickly."

That cooled their mirth, as he had intended it should. The laugh had been good for easing the disquiet, and perhaps more than disquiet, that had fallen over them all since they entered the mountains, but they must be ever mindful of what they were about and where they were if they were to leave with their lives.

As the others sat or lay or even walked a bit to stretch their legs, Eldran reclined with his reins wrapped loosely about one hand. He had had his own difficulties in keeping his mind cleanly on his purpose in the Kezankians. Even through the unease that hung about him like a miasma, a tall Zamoran beauty with arrogance enough for a score of kings had a way of intruding on his thoughts when he was not careful. But was she truly Zamoran, he wondered. Her manner, acting as if she ruled whatever ground she stood on, said yes. But those eyes. Like the mists of morning clinging to the oaks of the forest. No Zamoran ever had such eyes, as gray as his own.

Angrily he reminded himself of his purpose, to avenge his brother and those who went with him into the Kezankians, never to return. And to avenge as well those who had died attempting to defend their farmholds against the beast of fire. To make certain that more deaths did not come from the beast. If he and every man with him died, it would be small price for success. They had all agreed to that before ever they left Brythunia.

A raven circled high above him. Like the bird he and Jondra had shot, he thought. Angrily he leaped to his feet. Could nothing put the woman from his mind? Well, he would not be reminded of her longer by that accursed bird. He pulled his bow from its wolf-hide case behind his saddle.

"Eldran!" From a space clear of boulders higher on the mountain, a bony man with a pointed nose waved to him frantically. "Come quickly, Eldran!"

"What is it, Fyrdan?" Eldran called back, but he was scrambling up the slope as he spoke. Fyrdan was not one to become excited over nothing. Others of the band followed.

"There," the bony man said, flinging out an arm to point as Eldran joined him.

Eldran cupped his hands beside his eyes to improve his seeing, but there was little to make out save boiling dust and the tiny figures of struggling men on the hills far below. "Hillmen," he said finally.

"And Zamorans," Fyrdan added. "I saw the banner their general carried go down."

Slowly Eldran's hands dropped to his sides. "Forgive me, Jondra," he said softly.

"Perhaps the soldiers had not fetched her yet," Haral said. "Perhaps these are the other soldiers we saw."

Eldran shook his head. "The others were further west. And I watched their camp until their general left to find her."

"A Zamoran wench," Fyrdan said scornfully. "There are plenty of good Brythunian women eager for a tumble with. . . ." His words trailed off under Eldran's glare.

"We will speak no more of the woman," the gray-eyed man said. "We will talk of other things, things that must be said. We have tracked the beast here to its home ground, and its spoor is on the mountains themselves. The very rocks are baneful, and the air reeks of maleficence. Let no man say he has not felt it as I have."

"Next you will be claiming second sight," Haral grumbled, then added with a chuckle, "Unless you've changed greatly since last we swam together, you cannot qualify to become a priestess." No one echoed his jollity; grave eyes watched Eldran, who went on in grim tones.

"I have no need of second sight to scent death. Who follows me from here must resign himself that his bones will go unanointed. I will not think ill of any man who turns back, but let him do it now."

"Do you turn back?" Haral asked gently. Eldran shook his head. "Then," the plump man said, "I will not either. I am old enough to choose the place of my dying, an it comes to that."

"My brother rode with yours, Eldran," Fyrdan said. "My blood burns as hot for vengeance as yours."

One by one the others made it known that they, too, would go on, and Eldran nodded.

"Very well," he said simply. "What will come, will come. Let us ride."

The raven was gone, he saw as he made his way back down to the trail. Birds of ill omen, they were, yet he could not find gladness in him for its absence. It had reminded him of Jondra, and whether she lived or no he could not think he would ever see her again. But then, he thought bleakly, there would be ravens beyond counting deeper in the Kezankians, and bones aplenty for them to pick.

Chapter 14

Basrakan Imalla stalked the floor of his oaken-
paneled chamber with head bowed as if his multi-hued
turban were too heavy. His blood-red robes swirled
with the agitation of his pacing. So many worries
weighing on his shoulders, he thought. The path of
holiness was not an easy one. There was the matter of
another dead raven in the next chamber. Men, it had
said before dying. But how many, and where? And to
have two of the birds slain in only a few days. Did
someone know of the ravens' function? Someone
inimical to him? Another had reported men as well.
Not soldiers; the birds could distinguish them. But
the inability to count meant there could be ten or a
hundred. It might even be the same party seen by the
dead raven. He would have to increase his patrols
and find these interlopers, however many groups of
them there were.

At least the bird that accompanied the men he had
sent against the soldiers had reported victory. No, not

merely victory. Annihilation. But even with that came burdens. The warriors he had sent forth camped now, so said the raven. Squabbling among themselves over the looting of the dead, no doubt. But they would return. They had to. He had given them a victory, a sign from the old gods.

Unbidden the true source of his worries rushed back to mock him, though he tried as he had so often in days past to force it from him. A sign from the old gods. The sign of the ancient gods' favor. Seven times, now, he had tried to summon the drake, each attempt carefully hidden from the eyes even of his own acolytes, and seven times he had failed. Unrest grew in the camps for the lack of the showing. And those he had sent after the Eyes of Fire had not returned. Could the old gods have withdrawn their grace from him?

Wrapping his arms around him, he rocked back and forth on his heels. "Am I worthy, O gods of my forefathers?" he moaned. "Am I truly worthy?"

"Our question exactly, Imalla," a voice growled.

Basrakan spun, and blinked to find three hillmen confronting him. He struggled to recover his equilibrium. As he drew himself up, two of the bearded men shrank back. "You dare disturb me?" he rasped. "How did you pass my guards?"

The man who had stood his ground, his mustaches curled like the horns of a bull, spoke. "Even among your guards there are doubts, Imalla."

"You are called Walid," Basrakan said, and a flicker of fear appeared in the other's black eyes.

There were no sorceries involved, though. This Walid had been reported to him as one of the troublemakers, the questioners. It had taken him a moment to remember the man's description. He had not thought the troublemaking had gone so far as this, however. But he had prepared for every eventuality.

With false calmness he tucked his hands into the long sleeves of his crimson robe. "What doubts do *you* have, Walid?"

The man's thick mustache twitched at the repetition of his name, and he half turned his head as if looking for support from his companions. They remained well behind him, meeting neither his eyes nor Basrakan's. Walid drew a deep breath. "We came here, many of us, because we heard the old gods favored you. Those who came before us speak of a fabulous beast, a sign of that favor, but I have seen no such creature. What I *have* seen is thousands of hillmen sent to battle Zamoran soldiers, who have ever before slaughtered us when we fought them in numbers. And I have seen none of those warriors return."

"That is all?" Basrakan asked.

His suddenly mild tone seemed to startle Walid. "Is it not enough?" the mustached man demanded.

"More than enough," Basrakan replied. Within his sleeves his hands clasped small pouches he had prepared only a day past, when the unrest among the gathered tribes first truly began to worry him. Now he praised his foresight. "Much more than enough, Walid."

Basrakan's hands came out of his sleeves, and in a continuous motion he scattered the powder from one pouch across Walid. As the powder struck, the Imalla's right hand made arcane gestures, and he chanted in a tongue dead a thousand years.

Walid stared down at his chest in horror for a moment as the chilling incantation went on, then, with a shout of rage and fear, he grabbed for his tulwar. Even as his hand touched the hilt, though, fire spurted from his every pore. Flame surrounded him as clothes and hair turned to ash. His roar of anger became a shrill shriek of agony, then the hiss of boiling grease. A plume of oily black smoke rose from the collapsing sack that had been a man.

The other two men had stood, eyes bulging with terror, but now one burst for the door, and the other fell to his knees crying, "Forgiveness, Imalla! Forgiveness!"

In two quick strides Basrakan was on them, throwing the powder over the fleeing man and the kneeling one alike. His long-fingered hands gestured, and the chant rose once more. The running man made it to the door before fire engulfed him. The other fell on his face, wriggling toward Basrakan, then he, too, was a living pyre. Their screams lasted only moments, blending into a shrill whistle as flame consumed their bones.

At last even the black smoke guttered out. Only small heaps of dark, oily ash were left on the floor, and sooty smudges on the ceiling. The fierce-eyed Imalla viewed the residues of his accusers with satisfaction, but it faded quickly to grim anger. These men would have brothers, cousins, and nephews, scores of male relatives who, while they might fear to confront Basrakan openly, would most certainly now be a source of further dissention. Some might even go beyond words. The tribesmen lived and died by the blood feud, and nothing could turn them from it save death.

"So be it," he pronounced intently.

Dark face as cold and calm as if he had a lifetime for the task, Basrakan gathered a sampling from each pile of ash, scraping them into folded scraps of parchment with a bone knife four times blessed in rites before the ancient gods of the Kezankians. Ash from each dead man went into a thick-walled mortar of plain, unworked gold. The sorcerer's movements quickened as he added further ingredients, for speed now was essential. Powdered virgin's eye and ground firefly. Salamanders' hearts and the dried blood of infants. Potions and powders, the ingredients of which he dared not even think of. With the thigh bone of a woman strangled by her own daughter he ground the mixture, twelve times widdershins, intoning the hidden names of the ancient gods, names that chilled the marrow and made vapors of frost hang in the air. Twelve times the other way. Then it was done, this first step, leaving the golden vessel filled almost to the brim with black powder that seemed to swirl like smoke in its depths.

Gingerly, for the blending was deadly to the touch now, Basrakan carried the mortar to a cleared space on the pale stone floor. There, dipping a brush tipped with virgins' eyelashes into the moist mixture, he carefully scribed a precise pattern on the smooth stone. It was a cross, its arms of equal length exactly aligned to north and south, east and west. Tipping each arm was a circle, within which he drew the four idiograms of the ancient gods, the secret signs of earth, air, water, and fire. Next a triangle, its apex at the meeting of the arms of the cross, enclosed the symbol for the spirits of fire, and that same character was placed on each point of the triangle.

Basrakan paused, staring at what he had wrought, and his breath came fast. He would not admit to fear despite a tightening in his bowels, but this was more dangerous than anything he had yet attempted. An error in any phase, one completed or one to come, and the rite would rebound on him. Yet he knew there was no turning back.

Deftly he tipped the last of the powder into a silver censer on the end of a silver chain. Ordinary flint and steel provided the spark and set it smouldering. Aligning his feet carefully on the broad base of the triangle, he swung the censer in an intricate pattern. Wisps of smoke wafted upward from the silver ball, and Basrakan's incantation rose with the odoriferous vapors. With each swing of the censer one crystalline word rang in the air, words that even the fiery-eyed Imalla could not hear, for they were not meant for human ears, and the human mind could not comprehend them.

Around him the very air seemed to glisten darkly. Smoke from the censer thickened and fell to the stone floor, aligning itself unnaturally with the pattern drawn there. Basrakan's chant came faster, and more loudly. The words pealed hollowly, like funereal tolling from the depths of a cavern. Within the ropes of smoke now covering the configuration came a glow, ever fiercer and hotter, till it seemed as if all the fires of the earth's bowels were bound in those roiling thongs of black. Sweat rolled down Basrakan's thin cheeks from the heat. The glow became blinding, and his words rose higher and higher, the walls shivering under their impact.

Suddenly Basrakan ceased his cry. Silence came, and in that instant, glow and smoke and drawn pattern all vanished. Even the smoke from the censer failed.

Done, Basrakan thought. Weariness filled him. Even his bones felt weak. But what had had to be done, had been done.

A tremor shook him as his eye fell on the remains of his accusers. On each pile of ash, from which all that could be burned had been burned, danced pale flames. Even as he watched they licked into extinction. He drew a deep breath. This was no cause for fear, but rather for exaltation.

Jbeil burst into the chamber, panting, with one hand pressed hard to his side. "The bless . . . the bless . . . the blessings. . . ."

"An Imalla must be dignified," Basrakan snapped. Returning confidence, returning faith, washed away the dregs of his fear. "An Imalla does not run."

"But the camps, Imalla," Jbeil managed past gulps of air. "Fire. Men are burning. Burning, Imalla! Warriors, old men, boys. Even babes unweaned, Imalla! They simply burst into flame, and not water or dirt can extinguish them. Hundreds upon hundreds of them!"

"Not so many, I think," Basrakan replied coolly. "A hundred, perhaps, or even two, but not so many as you say."

"But, Imalla, there is panic."

"I will speak to the people, Jbeil, and calm them. Those who died were of tainted blood. Did the means of their dying tell you nothing?"

"The fire, Imalla?" Jbeil said uncertainly. "They offended the spirits of fire?"

Basrakan smiled as if at a pupil who had learned his lesson well. "More than offended, Jbeil. Much more. And all males of their blood shared their atonement." A thought struck him, a memory of words that seemed to have been spoken days in the past. "My guards, Jbeil. Did you see them as you came in?"

"Yes, Imalla. As I came to you. The two who were at your door accompanied Ruhallah Imalla on some errand." His eyes took on a sly cast. "They ran, Imalla. Ruhallah knows little of dignity. Only the urgency of my message brought me to such haste."

"Ruhallah had his own urgency," Basrakan said

so softly he might have been speaking to himself. He fixed the other man with an eye like a dagger. "Ruhallah is to blame for the fiery deaths this day. He and those false guards who flee with him. Ruhallah led those men of the blood that perished this day into false beliefs and tainted ways." It could be so, he thought. It must be so. Assuredly, it *was* so. "Ruhallah and the guards who flee with him must be brought back to face payment for what they have done." Few things amused Basrakan, but the next thought to visit him brought a smile to his thin lips. "They are to be given to the women of the men who died by fire this day. Let those who lost kith and kin exact their vengeance."

"As you command, Imalla, so will it be." Jbeil froze in a half-bow, and his eyes went wide. "Aaiee! Imalla, it had been driven from my mind by the burnings and. . . ." Basrakan glared at him, and he swallowed and went on. "Sharmal has returned, Imalla. One of those you sent after the Eyes of Fire, Imalla," he added when the tall holy man raised a questioning eyebrow.

"They have returned?" Basrakan said, excitement rising in his voice. "The Eyes of Fire are mine! All praise to the old gods!" Abruptly he was coldly calm, only an intensity of tone remaining of the emotion that had filled his speech. "Bring the gems to me. Immediately, fool! Nothing should have kept you from that. Nothing! And bring the men, as well. They will not find their rewards small."

"Imalla," Jbeil said hesitantly, "Sharmal is alone,

and empty handed. He babbles that the rest are dead, and other things, as well. But there is little of sense in any of it. He . . . he is mad, Imalla.''

Basrakan ground his teeth, and tugged at his forked beard as if he wanted to pull it out by the roots. ''Empty handed,'' he breathed at last, hoarse and icy. He could not be cheated of his desires now. He *would* not be. ''What occurred, Jbeil? Where are the Eyes of Fire? I will know these things. Put this Sharmal to the question. Strip him of his skin. Sear him to the bone. I will have answers!''

''But, Imalla,'' Jbeil whispered, ''the man is mad. The protection of the old gods is on him.''

''Do as I command!'' Basrakan roared, and his acolyte flinched.

''As . . . as you command, Imalla, so will it be.'' Jbeil bowed deeply, and moved backwards toward the door.

So much had happened, Basrakan thought, in such a short time. There was something he was forgetting. Something. . . . ''Jbeil!'' The other man jerked to a halt. ''There are strangers in the mountains, Jbeil. They are to be found, and any survivors brought to me for offering to the true gods. Let it be done!'' He gestured, and Jbeil nearly ran from the room.

Chapter 15

"We will make camp now." Jondra announced while the sun still rose. Arvaneus' voice rose, echoing her command, and obediently her hunters dismounted and began seeing to the pack animals and their own mounts.

Conan caught her eye questioningly, and she favored him with a smile. "When hunting a rare animal," she said, "care must be taken not to bypass its feeding grounds. We will spend days in each camp, searching."

"Let us hope this animal is not also searching," Conan replied. The noblewoman frowned, but before she could speak Arvaneus came to stand at her stirrup.

"Do you wish the trackers out now, my lady?" he asked.

Jondra nodded, and a shiver of excitement produced effects to draw male eyes. "It would be wonderful to get a shot at my quarry on the first day. Yes, Arvaneus. Put out your best trackers."

She looked expectantly at Conan, but he pretended not to notice. His tracking skill was the equal of any of the hunters', but he had no interest in finding the creature Jondra sought. He wanted only to see the two women returned to the safety of Shadizar, and he could offer them no protection if he was out tracking.

Jondra's face fell when Conan did not speak, but the dark-eyed huntsman smiled maliciously. "It takes a great special skill to be a tracker," he said to no one in particular. "My lady." He made an elegant bow to Jondra, then backed away, calling as he straightened. "Trackers out! Telades! Zurat! Abu!" His list ran on, and soon he and nine others were trotting out of the camp in ten different directions. They went afoot, for the slight spoor that a tracker must read as a scribe read words on parchment could be missed entirely from the back of a horse.

With the trackers gone, the beauteous noblewoman began ordering the placement of the camp, and Conan found a place to settle with a honing stone, a bit of rag and a vial of olive oil. A sword must be tended to, especially if it would soon find use, and Conan was sure his blade would not be idle long. The mountains seemed to overhang them with a sense of foreboding, and something permeated the very stones that made him uneasy. The honing stone slid along his blade with quiet sussuration. Morning grew into afternoon.

The camp, Conan decided after a time, was placed as well as it could be under the circumstances. The stunted trees that were scattered so sparsely through the Kezankians were in this spot gathered into what might pass for a grove, though an exceedingly thin one. At least they added some modicum to the hiding of the camp.

Jondra's scarlet tent, which she had never considered leaving behind, stood between two massive granite boulders and was screened from behind by the brown rock of a sheer cliff. No other tents had been brought—for which small favor the Cimmerian was grateful—and the hunters' blankets were scattered in twos and threes in a score of well-hidden depressions. The horses were picketed in a long, narrow hollow that could be missed even by a man looking for it. To one unfamiliar with the land the encampment would be all but invisible. The trouble, he thought sourly, was that the hillmen were more than familiar with their mountains. There would be trouble.

As though his thought of trouble had been a signal, a sound sliced through the cool mountain air, and Conan's hand stopped in the act of oiling his sword blade. Through the jagged peaks echoed a shrill, ululating cry, piercing to the bone and the heart. He had never heard the like of that sound, not from the throat of any man or any creature.

The big Cimmerian was not alone in being disturbed by the hunting call—for such he was sure it was. Hunters sat up in their blankets, exchanging worried glances. Some rose to walk a few paces, eyes searching the steep, encircling slopes. Jondra came to the flap of her tent, head tilted questioningly, listening. She wore leather now, jerkin and breeches, as always fitting her curves like a second skin, but plain brown, suitable for the hunt. When the sound was not repeated she retreated inside once more.

"What in Mitra's thrice-blessed name was that?" Tamira said, dropping into a crouch near Conan. She adjusted her short white robe to provide a modicum of decency, and wrapped slim arms about her knees. "Can it be the creature Jondra hunts?"

"I would not be surprised if it was," Conan said. He returned to the oiling of his blade. "Little good those rubies will do you if you end in the belly of that beast."

"You try to talk me into fleeing," she retorted, "leaving you with a clear path to the gems."

"I have told you," he began, but she cut him off.

"A clear path to Jondra's sleeping furs, then."

Conan sighed and slid his broadsword into his sheath. "You were in my arms this night past, and she not for two days. And I said that I came into these thrice-accursed mountains for you. Do you now call me liar?"

Her eyes slid away from his, to the rugged spires of granite surrounding them. "Do you think the trackers will find it? This beast, I mean? Perhaps, if they do not, we will leave these mountains. I would as well steal the rubies while returning to Shadizar."

"I would as soon they found naught but sore feet," Conan said. He remembered the half-charred fragment of skull and horn. "This beast will not be so easy to slay as Jondra believes, I fear. And you will not steal the rubies."

"So you *do* mean to take them yourself."

"I do not."

"Then you intend to save them for your paramour. For Jondra."

"Hannuman's Stones, woman! Will you give over?"

Tamira eyed him sharply. "I do not know whether I want you to be lying or not."

"What do you mean by that?" he asked in puzzlement.

"I intend to steal the rubies, you understand, no matter what you say or do." Her voice tightened. "But if you did not come for the rubies, then you came for me. Or for Jondra. I am uncertain whether I wouldn't rather have the sure knowledge that all you wanted was the gems."

Conan leaned back against the boulder behind him and laughed until he wheezed. "So you don't believe me?" he asked finally.

"I've known enough men to doubt anything any of you says."

"You have?" he exclaimed in feigned surprise. "I would have sworn I was the very first man you'd known."

Color flooded her cheeks, and she leaped to her feet. "Just you wait until—"

Whatever her threat was to be, Conan did not hear its finish, for Telades hurried into the camp, half out of breath and using his spear as a walking staff. Men hastened to surround him, and the Cimmerian was first among them.

A hail of words came from the hunters.

"Did you find tracks?"

"We heard a great cry."

"What did you see?"

"It must have been the thing we hunt."

"Did you see the beast?"

Telades tugged off his spiked helm and shook his shaved head. "I heard the cry, but I saw neither animal nor tracks."

"Give your report to me," Jondra snapped. The hunters parted to let her through. Her eagerness was betrayed by the bow in her hand. "Or am I to wait until you've told everyone else?"

"No, my lady," Telades replied abashedly. "I ask forgiveness. What I saw was the army, my lady. Soldiers."

Again a torrent of questions broke over the man.

"Are you sure?"

"From the lot we saw fighting?"

"How could they get into the mountains ahead of us?"

Jondra's cool gray eyes swept across the assembled hunters, and the torrent died as though she had cracked a whip.

"Where are those soldiers, Telades?" Conan asked. Jondra looked at him sharply, but closed her mouth and said nothing.

"Not two leagues to the north and east of us," Telades replied. "Their general is Lord Tenerses. I got close enough to see him, though they did not see me."

"Tenerses," Conan mused. "I have heard of him."

"They say he hunts glory," the shaven-headed hunter said, "but it seems he thinks well enough to know when danger is about. His camp is so well hidden, in a canyon with but one entrance, that I found it only by merest chance. And I could not see how many men he has with him."

"Not one fewer than Zathanides," Conan said, "if what I have heard of him is true. He is a man with a sense of his own importance, this Tenerses."

Jondra broke in in flat tones. "If you two are quite finished discussing the army, I would like to hear the results I sent this man for in the first place. Did you find tracks, Telades, or did you not?"

"Uh, no, my lady. No tracks."

"There are still nine others," the noblewoman said half to herself. "As for these soldiers," she went on in a more normal tone, "they have naught to do with us, and we naught to do with them. I see no reason why they should be a subject of further discussion, nor why they should even become aware of our existence. Am I understood?"

Her gaze was commanding as it met each man's eyes in turn, and each man mumbled assent and grew intent in his study of the ground beneath his feet, until she came to Conan. Eyes of chilling azure looked back at her in unblinking calmness, and it was smoky gray orbs that dropped to break the mesmerizing contact.

When she looked at him again, it was through long eyelashes. "I must talk with you, Conan," she murmured. "In my tent. I . . . would have your advice on the hunt."

Over Jondra's shoulder Conan saw Tamira watching him intently, hands on hips. "Perhaps later," he said. When the noblewoman blinked and stared, he added quickly, "The mountains are dangerous. We cannot spare even one watcher." Before she could say more—and he could see from the sparks in her eyes that she intended to say *much* more—he retreated across the camp to his place by the boulder.

As he settled once more with his back to the stone, he noticed that both women were looking at him. And both were glaring. The old saying was certainly proving true, he thought. He who has two women oft finds himself in possession of none. And not one thing could he think to do about it. With a sigh he set back to tending his steel. Some men claimed their blades had the personalities of women, but he had never known a sword to suffer jealousy.

The other trackers began returning at decreasing intervals. Jondra allowed these no time to become involved in extraneous—to her—matters with the other hunters. She met each man as he entered the camp, and her sharp gaze kept the rest back until she finished her questioning and gave the tracker leave to go.

One by one the trackers returned, and one by one they reported . . . nothing of interest to Jondra. One, who had searched near Telades, had found the cheekpiece of a soldier's helmet. Another had seen a great mountain ram with curling horns as long as a man's arm. Jondra angrily turned her back on him before he finished telling of it. Several saw hillmen, and in numbers enough to make a prudent man wary, but none had found the spoor of the beast, or anything that might remotely be taken as a sign of its presence or passage. The gray-eyed noblewoman heard each man out, and strode away from each impatiently tapping her bow against her thigh.

The last to return was Arvaneus, trotting into the camp to lean on his spear with an arrogant smile.

"Well?" Jondra demanded as she stalked up to him. "I suppose you have seen nothing either?"

The hawkfaced huntsman seemed taken aback at her tone, but he recovered quickly and swept a bow before her. "My lady, what you seek, I give to you." He shot a challenging look at Conan as he straightened. "*I*, Arvaneus, son of Lord Andanezeus, give it to you."

"You have found it?" Excitement brightened her face. "Where, Arvaneus?"

"A bare league to the east, my lady. I found the marks of great claws as long as a man's hand, and followed them for some distance. The tracks were made this day, and there cannot be another creature in these mountains to leave such spoor as human eyes have never before seen."

The entire camp stared in amazement as Jondra leaped spinning into the air, then danced three steps of a jig. "It must be. It must. I will give you gold to make you wealthy for this, Arvaneus. Find this beast for me, and I will give you an estate."

"I want no gold." Arvaneus said huskily, his black eyes suddenly hot. "Nor estates."

Jondra froze, staring at him, then turned unsteadily away. "Prepare horses," she commanded. "I would see these tracks."

The huntsman looked worriedly at the sky. The sun, giving little warmth in these mountains, lay halfway to the western horizon from its zenith. "It is late to begin a hunt. In the morning, at first light—"

"Do you question my commands?" she snapped. "I am no fool to start a hunt for a dangerous beast with night approaching, but I will see those tracks. Now! Twenty men. The rest will remain in camp and prepare for the hunt tomorrow."

"As you command, my lady," Arvaneus muttered. He glared malevolently at Conan as Jondra turned to the big Cimmerian and spoke in a soft voice.

"Will you ride with me, Conan? I . . . I would feel much safer." The awkwardness of her words and the coloring of her cheeks gave her the lie. With obvious difficulty, she added, "Please?"

Wordlessly Conan rose and walked to the picket line. Arvaneus barked orders, and others joined the Cimmerian. As Conan was fastening his saddle girth, he became aware of Tamira, making a great show of idly petting the nose of a roan next to his tall black.

"Will you ride with me, Conan?" she mimicked softly. "I will feel *so* much safer." She twisted up her face as if to spit.

Conan let out a long breath. "I'd not like to see

either of you dead, or a hillman's slave. You will be safer here than will she out there, so I go with her.''

He stepped up into the high-pommeled Zamoran saddle. Tamira trotted alongside as he rode from the hollow where the horses were picketed. ''You will be out there,'' she told him, ''and so will she. You could return to find me gone, Conan. And the rubies. What is to keep me here?''

''Why, you'll be waiting for me,'' he laughed, booting his mount to a trot. A hurled rock bounced off his shoulder, but he did not look back.

Chapter 16

The party of Zamoran hunters made their way in single file along the gullies and clefts that lined the mountains like wrinkles of ancient age on the face of the earth. Arvaneus led, since he knew the way, and Jondra rode close behind him. Conan, in turn, kept close to the tall noblewoman. There would be little time to spare when protection was needed. The mountains seemed to press in on them malignly, even when their way opened enough for a score of men or more to ride abreast.

The big Cimmerian's eyes searched the jagged crags and steep slopes around them constantly, and with instincts long buried in civilized men he probed for his enemies. No sign of hillmen did he see, no hint of them came to his senses, but menace still oozed from the stones. Outwardly he seemed at ease, but he was dry tinder waiting for a spark.

Abruptly Arvaneus drew rein where the walls of rock were steep and close. "There, my lady," the

huntsman said, pointing to the ground. "Here is the
first track I found."

Jondra scrambled from her saddle to kneel by a
small patch of clay. The deep marks of two massive
claws and part of a third were impressed there. "It is
larger than I thought," she murmured, running two
slender fingers into one impression.

"We have seen the tracks," Conan said. The op-
pressive air seemed thicker to him. "Let us return to
the camp."

Arvaneus' lip curled in a sneer. "Are you afraid,
barbar? My lady, there are more tracks further on.
Some are complete."

"I must see that," Jondra exclaimed. Swinging
into her saddle she galloped ahead, and Arvaneus
spurred after her.

Conan exchanged a look with Telades—by the
shaven-headed hunter's sour face he liked this as
little as the Cimmerian—then they and the rest of the
column of horsemen followed.

As it had often before, the narrow passage opened
out. This time it led into a small canyon, perhaps a
hundred paces wide, with five narrow draws cutting
its steep brown walls. Conan eyed those openings
suspiciously. Any enemy hidden in those would be
on them before they had time to react. The hillmen's
favorite tactic was the ambush.

On the floor of the canyon the spoor of the beast
was plentiful. Tracks leading both in and out showed
that the beast had explored the narrow cuts. Unease
permeated the column; hunters shifted their spears

nervously, or reached back to touch the cased bows behind their saddles, and horses danced and shied. Jondra uncased her bow as she dismounted at the track Arvaneus pointed out, and nocked an arrow before kneeling to examine it. The hawk-faced huntsman frowned at the ground around him, attempting with only partial success to control his mount's quick sidesteps.

Conan found himself wondering about that frown. Arvaneus had seen this canyon and the tracks that filled it only a short time before. What was there for him to frown about? The big Cimmerian's breath caught in his throat. Unless there were *more* tracks than he had seen before. If that was true they must leave immediately.

Conan opened his mouth, and a shrill ululation split the air, chilling the blood, making the horses buck and scream. Jondra's mount tore the reins from her hands and bolted, nostrils flaring and eyes rolling wildly, leaving the noblewoman standing like a statue of ice. With difficulty the Cimmerian pulled his big black around. "Crom," he breathed into the din filling the stone walls.

Into the canyon came a monstrous creature, huge, on massive legs. Multi-hued scales glittered in the sinking sun, broken only by dark, leathery-appearing bulges on its back. Adamantine claws gouged the stone beneath them. The broad head was thrown back, the widespread maw revealing jagged teeth like splinters of stone, and that piercing cry struck men to their souls.

The hunters were men who had faced death many times, and if it had never before confronted them in such form, still death was no stranger to them. As that malevolent howl ended they forced themselves into movement, fighting horses half-mad with terror to spread and surround the gargantuan form. The man nearest the beast leveled his spear like a lance and charged. With a clang as of steel against stone the spear struck, and the rider was shivered from his saddle. The great head lowered, and flame roared from that gaping mouth. Man and horse shrieked as one, a shrillness that never seemed to end, as they were roasted alive.

A gasp rose from the other hunters, but they were already launching their attack, men charging in from from either flank. Even had they wished to turn aside, the beast gave them no chance. More swiftly than any leopard it moved, claws sweeping bloody rags that had once been men to the ground, jaws crushing men and horses alike. Spears splintered like straws against the iridescent scales, and the cries of the dying drowned out all save thought, and fear became the only thought in the hunter's minds.

Through that howling maelstrom of certain death Conan galloped, swinging low out of his saddle to snatch an unbroken spear from the bloody ground. Those great golden eyes, he thought. The eyes had to be vulnerable, or the long, dark protuberances on its back. He forced his mount to turn—it struggled to run on, away from the horror—and the sight that met his eyes sent a quiver through him as not even the beast's hunting cry had.

Jondra stood not ten paces from the creature's head. Even as he saw her, an arrow left her bow. Squarely on one malevolent golden eye the shaft struck. And ricocheted away. The beast lunged, claws streaking toward her. Frantically she leaped back, but the tip of one claw snagged in the laces of her red leather jerkin, and she was jerked into the air to dangle before the creature's eyes. Ignoring the carnage around it, the shouting, screaming men, the beast seemed to study her.

A thrill of horror coursed through Conan. There was a light of intelligence in those auric globes. But if the brain behind them could reason, it was a form of reasoning too inhuman for the mind of man to know it. It did not see the beautiful woman as other than prey. The spike-toothed mouth opened, and Jondra was drawn closer.

Conan's spear came up. "Crom!" he bellowed, and his heels thudded his fear-ridden mount into a charge. His spearpoint held steady on one leathery bulge. He clamped his knees tightly on the animal against the shock he had seen throw others to the ground, but even so the force of the blow rocked through him, staggering his horse to its knees.

With sinuous grace and blinding speed the glittering beast twisted, smashing Conan with the leg from which Jondra dangled. Breath rushed from the big Cimmerian as he was lifted and hurled through the air. Stony ground rushed up to slam what little air remained from his chest. Desperately he fought to breathe, forced numbed muscles to move, rolled to hands and knees, staggered to his feet. Jondra lay on her back near him, writhing, bare breasts heaving as she struggled for air.

The beast turned its attention to the Cimmerian, Jondra's jerkin still tangled in its claws. What remained of his horse lay quivering beneath the creature; gobbets of flesh fell from its fanged jaws.

In what he knew was a futile gesture Conan drew his ancient broadsword. Steel made no mark on those infrangile scales. He could not move quickly enough to escape the creature's attack unburdened, much less carrying Jondra, and he could not leave her behind. Yet he would not die without fighting.

"Ho, Conan!" Swaying in his saddle, Telades rode toward the beast from behind. The mail over his chest was rent, and blood drenched him, but he gripped his spear firmly. "Get her away, northlander!" Pounding his boots into his horse's flanks, he forced it forward.

Iridescent scales flashed as the creature spun.

"No!" Conan shouted.

Flame engulfed the shaven-headed hunter, and the beast leaped to tear at smouldering flesh.

The Cimmerian would not waste Telades' sacrifice. Sheathing his blade, he scooped Jondra from the ground and darted into a narrow cleft, pursued by the sounds of crunching bone.

As the terrible grinding faded behind him, Jondra

stirred in his arms. "I did not mean for them to die," she whispered. Her eyes were horror-laden pools.

"You wanted to hunt the beast," he said, not slowing his steady stride. Under other circumstances he would have searched for survivors. Now he thought only of getting Jondra far from that charnel scene, back to the relative safety of the camp.

Jondra pressed herself more firmly against his broad chest as if sheltering from storm winds in the safety of a huge boulder. "Telades gave his life for me," she murmured, shivering. "Truly, I did not wish it to be. Oh, Conan, what can I do?"

Conan stopped dead, and she huddled in his arms as though hiding from his icy blue gaze. "Leave these mountains," he said harshly. "Go back to Shadizar. Forget this beast, and always remember the men who died for your foolishness and pride."

Anger and arrogance flared across her face. Her fist rose, then abruptly fell limp. Tears leaked down her cheeks. "I will," she wept. "Before all the gods, I swear it."

"It will not repay Telades' sacrifice," he said, "but it will at least mean that you value what he did."

Gently she touched Conan's cheek. "Never have I wanted a man to guide me, but you almost make me. . . ." Small white teeth bit her full underlip, and she dropped her eyes. "Will you come back to Shadizar with me?" she said softly, shifting in his grasp again so that her full, round breasts were exposed to his gaze.

"Perhaps," he replied gruffly, and began walking once more, with his full concentration on the twists of the cleft and the stony ground beneath his feet. Only a fool would refuse a woman like the one he held. And only a fool would disregard the advice he had given. But Telades had become a friend, and the man had died for him as well as for her.

A part of the Cimmerian's code demanded that Telades' death, offered in place of his own, should be repaid, just as another part of that code demanded that he see Jondra and Tamira to safety. At the moment the second seemed much more easily accomplished than the first! How, he thought, could he slay a beast that steel could not harm? If he took no notice of the charms Jondra displayed in his arms, it was no wonder.

Chapter 17

Tamira was the first person Conan saw when he
strode into the camp with his arms full of half-naked
noblewoman and the sun a bloody ball balanced on
jagged peaks. The slender young thief regarded him
with fists on hips and a jaundiced eye for the way
Jondra clung to him. Then Jondra looked around
dazedly, revealing her tear-stained face. Tamira's jaw
dropped, and she dashed into the red-walled tent to
return with a cloak.

As Conan stood Jondra upright, the smaller woman
enfolded her in soft blue wool. When he released his
hold on her, the noblewoman sank to her knees.
Tamira knelt beside her, drawing Jondra's head to
her shoulder and glaring up at the big Cimmerian.

"What happened?" she demanded hotly.

"We found the beast she hunts. Hunted. Have any
of the others returned?"

Dark eyes widening with sudden fear, Tamira shook

her head. "None. They . . . they could not all be dead?"

"Of course not," Conan said. He would be very surprised ever to see another of them alive, but there was no point in terrifying the wench more than she already was. Better to find work to occupy her mind. "See to her," he told Tamira. "She never stopped crying for a hundred paces together all the way back here."

"And no wonder," Tamira replied hotly, "with no better care than you've taken of her." She bundled the unresisting noblewoman off to her tent, leaving Conan standing open-mouthed.

He would never understand women, he decided. Never. Then he became aware of the remaining hunters gathered around him, looking at him worriedly. Looking to him for commands, he realized with some surprise. Firmly he put all thoughts of women from his mind.

"At dawn," he told them, "we leave for Shadizar. But first we must survive until then. No man sleeps tonight, unless he wants to risk waking with his throat cut. And no fires. Break open the supply packs."

With as much haste as Conan could manage, the hunters prepared themselves. All of the arrows were shared out, three quivers per man, and each man had an extra spear, as well as a waterbag and a pouch of dried meat. A coward or two might flee, with the means at hand, but he would not condemn the others to death if flight was required.

An assault from hillmen might come at any time, from any quarter save the cliff that backed Jondra's tent. Even if the first thrust were beaten off, they could not afford to be there when daylight came, pinned like bugs beneath a butcher bird's claws. They would attempt to retreat after an attack, or during, if it could not be driven back. And if they were on the point of being overwhelmed, every man would have to see to his own survival as best he could.

Worst of all would be an attack by the beast. As he moved through the darkening twilight from man to man, Conan left each with same final words. "Do not try to fight the beast. If it comes, run, and hope your gods feel kindly toward you."

Not far from Jondra's tent Conan settled into a flat-footed squat. Did the worst come, the others had only themselves to think of. He would need to be close to the women if he was to get them away.

A crunch of stone underfoot announced Tamira's approach, and he shifted his pair of spears to make a space for her.

"She's asleep," the slender woman sighed as she dropped to the ground beside him. "She wore herself out with tears. And who's to question it, after what she saw?"

"It happened by her command," Conan said quietly, "and for her pride. That Brythunian told her of the beast, and I told her what I had discovered of it."

"You are a hard man, Cimmerian. As hard as these mountains."

"I am a man," he told her simply.

For a time Tamira was silent. Finally she said, "Jondra says you are returning to Shadizar with her."

Conan gave a sour grunt. "It seems she talked a lot for a woman on the point of exhaustion."

"She plans to have apartments constructed for you in her palace."

"Ridiculous."

"She intends to dress you all in silk, with wristlets and armbands of gold to show off your muscles."

"What?" He thought he heard a giggle beside him in the deepening dark, and glared at her. "Enjoy your jokes, girl," he growled. "I, myself, do not find them funny."

"You were *her* first man, too, Conan. You cannot know what that means to a woman, but I do. She cares for you. Or perhaps it is for the image of you that she cares. She asked me if there were other men like you. She even compared you with Eldran, that Brythunian. She pretended not to remember his name, but she did."

Something in her voice struck him. "Mitra blind me if you don't pity her." His tone was incredulous.

"She knows less of men than I," the slender thief replied defensively. "It is a hard thing to be a woman in a world with men."

"It would be harder in a world without them," he said drily, and she fisted him in the ribs.

"I don't find *your* jokes," she began, but his hand closed over her mouth.

Intently he listened for the sound he was sure he

had heard before. There. The scrape of a hoof—an *unshod* hoof—on stone.

"Go to the tent," he whispered, giving her a push in the right direction. "Rouse her, and be ready to flee. Hurry!"

At that instant a cry broke the night. "By the will of the true gods!" And hordes of hillmen swarmed through the camp on shaggy mountain horses, curved tulwar blades gleaming in the pale moonlight as they rose and fell.

Conan hefted a spear and threw at the nearest target. A turbanned rider, transfixed, screamed and toppled from his galloping horse. Another hillman, calling loudly on his gods, closed with raised steel. There was no chance for the Cimmerian to throw his second spear. He dropped flat and swung it like a club at the legs of the charging animal. With a sharp crack the haft of the spear struck; horse and rider somersaulted. Before the hillman could rise, Conan put a forearm's length of spear through his chest.

All about the Cimmerian steel clanged against steel. Men shouted battle cries, shouted death rattles. In that deadly, bloody tempest an ingrained barbarian sense gave Conan warning. Pulling the spear free, he whirled in time to block a slashing tulwar. Deftly he rotated his spear point against the curved blade, thrust over it into his bearded attacker's throat. Dying, the hillman clutched the weapon that killed him with both hands. His horse ran out from under him, and as he fell he wrenched the spear from Conan's grip.

"Conan!" Tamira's shriek cut through the din to the Cimmerian's ears. "Conan!"

Desperately the Cimmerian's eyes sought for the slender woman . . . and found her, lifted to a hillman's saddle by a fist in her hair. Grinning broadly through his beard, the tribesman tauntingly lowered his blade toward her throat. With one hand she frantically attempted to fend off the razor edge, while the other clutched at his robes.

Conan's broadsword came into his hand. Two bounds took him to Tamira's side; the hillman's head went back, and his mouth fell open as the Cimmerian's steel slid smoothly between his ribs. Lifeless fingers loosened in Tamira's hair, and Conan caught her as she fell. Trembling arms snaked round his neck; she sobbed limply against his chest.

With a corpse on its back the horse galloped on, and in the space of a breath Conan had taken in the situation in the camp. The fight went badly. Had gone badly, for there was little of it left. Few of the turbanned warriors remained in the camp, and they were occupied with mutilating the dead. Murderous cries from the dark told of hillmen spreading in pursuit of hunters. Jondra's tent was in flames.

A chill went through the big Cimmerian. As he watched, the last of the tent collapsed, sending a shower of sparks into the night. If Jondra was in that, there was no hope for her. He hoped that she had gotten out, but he could not help her now. He had a woman to care for, and no time to spare for another.

Bending to catch Tamira behind the knees, he

heaved her onto his shoulder like a sack. A half-formed protest came through her weeping, but the flow of tears did not slow. None of the tribesmen slashing at corpses noticed the muscular youth or his well-curved burden as he faded into the night.

Like a spirit Conan moved from shadow to shadow. Darkness alone, however, was no shield, he knew. From the clouded velvet sky a nacreous moon shed little light, but enough to make movement plain to a discerning eye, and Tamira's short, white robe made matters no better. The night-clad rocks were filled with the clatter of galloping hooves on stone, the shouts of hunting hillmen. They hunted, and, given time, they would find.

The Cimmerian kept moving, always away from the noise of the hillmen, and his eyes searched for a hiding place. A line of deeper blackness within the dark caught his gaze. He made his way to it and found a horizontal fracture in the face of a cliff. It was wide enough to hold Tamira, deep enough for her to remain hidden from all but someone sticking an arm into it.

Lowering the girl from his shoulder, he thrust her into the crack. "Stay quiet," he told her in low tones, "and do not move. I'll be back as quickly as I can. Listen to me, woman!"

"He . . . he was going to kill me," she sobbed. "He was l-laughing." She clutched at him, but he gently removed her hands from his shoulders.

" 'Tis over, now. You are safe, Tamira."

"Don't leave me."

"I must find Jondra. Remain here till I return, and I will get the three of us out of these mountains." He had thought his voice full of confidence—certainly more confidence than he felt, at the moment—but she drew back from him into the crack in the cliff.

"Go then," she said sullenly. He could not see her, but her tears seemed to dry up suddenly. "Well? Go, if you want to."

He hesitated, but Jondra was still to be found, and whether alive or dead he did not know. Tamira would be safe here until he could return. "I will come back quickly," he said, and slipped away into the night.

Tamira peered from the crevice, but though her night vision was like that of a cat, she could see nothing. Conan had disappeared. She settled back sulkily.

She had nearly been killed, had been taunted with her own death, and he went after *her* when it should have been clear even to a blind man that she needed the comfort of his arms. But then, were not all men blind? It was not fair that he could affect her so much, while he cared so little. Once she had been able to think calmly and logically about any man. Once—it seemed a hundred years ago—before she allowed the young Cimmerian giant to. . . . Even alone in the dark she blushed at the thought.

She would not think of him any more, she decided. Drawing herself to the front of the crack, she tried once more to pierce the darkness. It was futile, like attempting to peer through a raven's wing. A chill wind whined through the mountains, and she pulled her knees up, huddling, painfully aware of how little warmth was to be had from her short tunic.

Where *had* he gone? To look for Jondra, he claimed, but how did he intend to find her in the night? Was the noblewoman even alive? The tent had been aflame, Tamira remembered. Nothing could have survived in that. Except . . . the iron chests containing Jondra's jewels.

Tamira's eyes gleamed with delight, and she bit her lip to suppress a giggle. "Let him search for Jondra," she whispered. "He'll return to find me gone. Gone from the mountains, and the rubies with me."

With the suppleness of a cat she rolled from the crevice, came to her feet in the night. The cold breeze ruffled her white tunic about her thighs. For an instant she considered the problem of that garment's paleness.

"Well, I cannot go naked," she said finally, then clamped her teeth shut. She could not afford to make a sound, now.

Silently she glided into the dark, moving with all the stealthy skill she possessed. No matter what was said in Shadizar, in the taverns of the Desert, concerning Conan, she *was* the best thief in the city.

A sound halted her, a grating as of boots on rock, and she wished she had her daggers. Whoever it was, she thought contemptuously, he was clumsy. Noiselessly she moved away from he-who-stepped-on-rocks

. . . and was buried beneath a rush of smelly robes
and unwashed flesh.

She kicked at the cursing men who swarmed over
her, struck at them until her wrists were caught in a
grip like a vise. Hands fumbled at her body. She saw
a bearded face, merciless and hard, and a curved
dagger raised high. A scream choked in her throat.
So many men to kill one woman. It was unfair, she
thought dully. Her tunic was grasped at the neck and
ripped open to the waist.

"See!" a voice said hoarsely. "It is as I said. A
woman, and young."

The hard face did not change. "A lowland woman!
A vessel of lust and corruption!"

"Even so," a third man said, "remember the
Imalla's commands. And remember Walid's fate before you think to disobey." The hard-faced man
blinked at that, and frowned.

"Take me to the Imalla," Tamira gasped. She
knew that Imallas were holy men among the hill
tribes. Surely a holy man would protect her.

The hard face split in an evil grin. "Let it be as the
wench wishes. Mayhap she will come to regret not
choosing my blade." And he began to laugh.

Chapter 18

In the canescent pre-dawn light Conan flattened himself on a narrow granite ledge as a file of hillmen rode by on a narrow path below, between steep walls. Their numbers had thinned as the night waned, but there were still too many of the bearded men to suit him. As the last of the horsemen disappeared up the twisting track, the big Cimmerian scrambled from fingerhold to fingerhold, down from the ledge, and set off at a trot in the opposite direction, toward the campsite that had become a bloody shambles so short a time before, toward Tamira's hiding place.

Two hundred paces down the trail he passed the remains of one of the Zamoran hunters. He could not tell which. The headless body, covered with blackened blood and bright green flies, lay with limbs twisted at unnatural angles. Conan gave the corpse not a glance as he went by. He had found too many others during the night, some worse than this, and at each one he had only been grateful it was not Jondra.

Now worry for Tamira filled his mind. He was sure she was safe—even in daylight that crack would not be easily noticed—but she had been alone for the entire night, a night filled with hillmen and the memories of murder.

Along the slope of a mountain he trotted, eyes ever watchful. Dropping to his belly, he crawled to the top of a rough stone outcropping. Below him lay the camp, blackened ground and ash where Jondra's tent had stood against the cliff. Half a score bodies, many in more than one piece, were scattered among the stunted trees—Zamoran bodies only, for the hillmen had carried their own dead away. There was no sound but the somber droning of flies.

Conan took a deep breath and went over the ridgetop, half sliding down the other side on loose rocks and shale. The dead he let lie, for he had no time to waste on burials or funeral rites. Instead he concentrated on what might be of use to the living. A spear, whole and overlooked by the hillmen. A waterbag unslashed and bulging damply. A pouch of dried meat.

The tribesmen had been thorough in their looting, however, and there was little to find. Broken spearpoints, the cook's pots, even the rope used for picketing horses had been taken, and the ashes of Jondra's tent had been sifted for anything not consumed by the flames. He did find his black Khauranian cloak, tucked where he had left it beneath the edge of a boulder. He added it to the pitiful pile.

"So you are a thief, a looter!"

At the hoarse words Conan grabbed up the spear and whirled. Arvaneus shuffled toward him, black eyes glittering, knuckles white on his spear haft. The huntsman's head was bare; dust covered him, and his baggy white breeches were torn.

"It is good to see another of Jondra's party alive," Conan said. "All thought you were slain by the beast."

The huntsman's eyes slid off to the side, skipped from body to body. "The beast," he whispered. "Mortal men could not face it. Any fool could see that. That cry. . . ." He shivered. "They should have fled," he went on plaintively. "That was the only thing to do. To try to fight it, to stay even a moment. . . ." His gaze fell on the pile Conan had made, and he tilted his head to look sidelong at the big Cimmerian. "So you are a thief, stealing from the Lady Jondra."

Hair stirred on the back of Conan's neck. Madness was not something he had encountered frequently, especially in one he had known when sane. "These supplies may save Jondra's life," he said, "when I find her. She is lost, Arvaneus. I must find her quickly if she is to get out of these mountains alive."

"So pretty," Arvaneus said softly, "with her long legs, and those round breasts meant to pillow a man's head. So pretty, my Lady Jondra."

"I am going now," Conan said, stretching out one hand to pick up his cloak. He was careful not to take his eyes from Arvaneus, for the other man still gripped his spear as if ready to use it.

"I watched her," the swarthy huntsman went on. The mad light in his eyes deepened. "Watched her run from the camp. Watched her hide from the hillmen. She did not see me. No. But I will go to her, and she will be grateful. She will know me for the man I am, not just as her chief huntsman."

Conan froze when he realized what Arvaneus was saying. The Cimmerian let out a long breath, and chose his words carefully. "Let us go to Jondra together. We can take her back to Shadizar, Arvaneus. She will be very grateful to you."

"You lie!" The huntsman's face twisted as if he was on the point of tears; his hands flexed on his spear haft. "You want her for yourself! You are not good enough to lick her sandals!"

"Arvaneus, I—"

Conan cut his words short as the huntsman thrust at him. Whipping his cloak up, the Cimmerian entangled the other man's spear point, but Arvaneus ripped his weapon free, and Conan was forced to leap back as gleaming steel lanced toward him once more. Warily, the two men circled, weapons at the ready.

"Arvaneus," Conan said, "there is no need for this." He did not want to kill the man. He needed to know where Jondra was.

"There is need for you to die," the hawkfaced man panted. Their spearpoints clattered as he felt for weakness and Conan deflected his probes.

"We have enemies enough around us," Conan told him. "We should not do their killing for them."

"Die!" Arvaneus screamed, rushing forward, spear outthrust.

Conan parried the thrust, but the huntsman did not draw back. He came on, straight onto the Cimmerian's spearpoint. Arvaneus' weapon dropped to the ground, but he took yet another step forward, clawed hands reached for Conan, impaling himself further. Surprise flooded his face; jerkily he looked down at the thick wooden shaft standing out from his chest.

The big Cimmerian caught Arvaneus as he collapsed, eased him to the stony ground. "Where is she?" Conan demanded. "Erlik blast you, where is Jondra?"

Laughter wracked the huntsman. "Die, barbar," he rasped. "Die." Blood welled up in his mouth, and he sagged, eyes glazing.

With a muttered curse Conan got to his feet. At least she was alive, he thought. If it was not all a fantasy constructed by a man mind. Gathering up his supplies, he set out for Tamira's hiding place.

From the shaded shelter of huge stone slabs, split from the cliff behind her by an earthquake centuries gone, Jondra stared longingly at the tiny pool of water far below and licked her lips. Had she known it was there while dark still covered the Kezankians, she would not have thought twice before assuaging her thirst. But now. . . . She peered to the east, to a sun still half-hidden by the jagged peaks. It was full enough light to expose her clearly to the eyes of any watchers.

And expose, the voluptuous noblewoman thought

wryly, was exactly the right word. Save for the dust of flight on her legs, she was quite naked.

"Not the proper dress for a noble Zamoran woman while hunting," she whispered to herself. But then, Zamoran nobles were seldom roused from their slumber by murderous hillmen or tents burning around them. Nor did they take part in the hunt as the prey.

She turned once more to study the pool, and licked lips that were dry again in moments. To reach it she would have to traverse a steep, rocky slope with not so much as a blade of grass for cover. At the bottom of the slope was a drop; she could not be sure how far from this angle, but it did not look enough to cause difficulty. The pool itself beckoned her enticingly. A patch of water she could doubtless wade in three strides without sinking to her knees, with three stunted trees on its edge, and at that moment it seemed more inviting than her palace gardens.

"I will not remain here until my tongue swells," she announced to the air. As if the sound of her own voice had spurred her to action, she crawled from the shelter of the stone slabs and started down the slope.

At first she moved carefully, picking her way over the loose stone. With every step, however, she became more aware of her nudity, of the way her breasts swayed with every movement, of how her skin flashed palely in the sunlight. First night and then the stone slabs had provided some illusion of being less naked. She had often lain naked in her garden, luxuriating in the warmth of the sun, but here sunlight stripped the illusion as bare as she. Here she could not know who watched her. Reason told her if there was a watcher, she had greater problems than nudity, but reason prevailed nothing against her feelings. Curling one arm over her breasts helped little, and she found herself crouching more and more, hurrying faster, taking less care of where she put her feet.

Abruptly the stones beneath her turned, and she was on her back, sliding amid a cloud of dust. Desperately she clawed for a hold, but each stone she grasped merely set others sliding. Just as she was ready to moan that matters could not get worse, she found herself falling. Only for long enough to be aware of the fall did she drop, then a jolt pulled her up short. The slide of rocks and dirt she had begun did not cease, however. A torrent of rubble showered down on her. Covering her face with her arms, spitting to clear dust from her mouth, she reflected that she would be a mass of bruises from shoulders to ankles after this day.

The rain of dirt and stones slowed and halted, and Jondra examined her position with a sinking feeling. The first shock was that she hung upside down, against the face of the drop she had been sure would present no difficulty. A twisted tree stump no thicker than her wrist held her ankle firmly in the V it formed with the face of the drop. Beneath her a pile of rubble from her fall reached just high enough for her to touch the stones with her fingertips.

Deliberately she closed her eyes and took three deep breaths to calm herself. There had to be a way out. She always found a way to get what she wanted, and she did *not* want to die hanging like a side of mutton. She would, she decided, just have to get hold of the stump and lift her ankle free.

At her first attempt to bend double a jolt of pain shot from her ankle, and she fell back gasping. The ankle was not broken, she decided. She would not accept that it was. Steeling herself against the pain, she tried again. Her fingers brushed the stump. Once more, she thought.

A rustle drew her eyes toward the pool, and terror chilled her blood. A bearded hillman stood there in filthy yellow tunic and stained, baggy trousers. He licked his lips slowly, and his staring black eyes burned with lust. He started toward her, already loosening his garments. Suddenly there was a noise like a sharp slap, and the hillman stopped, sank to his knees. Jondra blinked, then saw the arrow standing out from his neck.

Frantically she searched for the shaft's source. A movement on a mountain caught her eye, a moment's view of something that could have been a bow. Three hundred paces, the archer in her measured calmly, while the rest of her nearly wept for relief. Whichever of her hunters it was, she thought, she would gift him with as much gold as he could carry.

But she was not about to let anyone, least of all a man in her service, find her in such a helpless position. Redoubling her efforts, she split several splinters of wood from the stump and chipped her fingernails, but got no closer to freeing herself.

Suddenly she gasped in renewed horror at the sight of the man who appeared walking slowly toward her. This was no hillman, this tall form with fur leggings and clean-shaven face and gray eyes. She knew that face and the name that went with it, though she would have given much to deny it. Eldran. Vainly she tried to protect her modesty with her hands.

"You!" she spat. "Go away, and leave me alone!"

He continued his slow advance toward her, one hand resting lightly on the hilt of his broadsword, his fur-lined cloak slung back from his shoulders. No bow or quiver was in evidence. His eyes were fixed on her, and his face was grim.

"Stop staring at me!" Jondra demanded. "Go away, I tell you. I neither need nor want your help."

She flinched as three hillmen burst silently from the rocks behind the Brythunian, rushing at him with raised tulwars. Her mouth opened to scream . . . and Eldran whirled, the broadsword with its clawed quillons seeming to flow into his hand. In movements almost too fast for her to follow the four danced of death. Blood wetted steel. A bearded head rolled in the dust. And then all three hillmen were down, and Eldran was calmly wiping his blade on the cloak of one.

Sheathing the steel, he stepped closer to her. "Perhaps you do not want my help," he said quietly, "but you do need it."

Jondra realized her mouth was still open and snapped it shut. Then she decided silence would not do, but before she could speak the big Brythunian had stepped onto the pile of rubble, taken hold of her calves and lifted her clear of the stump that had held her. One arm went behind her knees, and she was swung up into his arms. He cradled her there as easily as did Conan, she thought. He was as tall as the Cimmerian, too, though not so broad across the shoulders. For the first time since the attack she felt safe. Color abruptly flooded her face as the nature of her thoughts became clear to her.

"Put me down," she told him. "I said, put me down!"

Silent, he carried her to the pool and lowered her gently by its edge. "You are down," he said. She winced as he felt her ankle. "A bad bruise, but it should heal in a few days."

There was dried blood on his forehead, she saw. "How came you by that? Have you met other hillmen?"

"I must get my bow," he said curtly, and stalked away.

As well if he did not return, she thought angrily, but the thought brought a twinge of anxiety. Suppose he did *not* return. Suppose he decided to abandon her, naked and alone in this wilderness. When he reappeared she gave a small sigh of relief, and then was angry with herself for that.

He set his bow and a hide quiver of arrows down, then turned to her with a bleak face. "We met other hillmen, yes. Two score men followed me into these accursed mountains, and I failed to keep them safe until we accomplished our purpose. Hillmen, hundreds of them, found our camp. I do not know if any of my companions still live." He sighed heavily. "I surmise the same fate befell you. I wish I could promise to see you to safety, but there is a task I have yet to accomplish, and it must take precedence even over you. I will do what I can for you, though. I must regret that I cannot take days to sit here and just look at you."

It came to her that he *was* looking at her, looking as if he intended to commit what he saw to memory. It also came to her that she was naked. Quickly she scrambled to her knees, crouching with her arms over her breasts. "A civilized man would turn his back," she snapped.

"Then the men you call civilized do not appreciate beauty in a woman."

"Give me your cloak," she commanded. "I am no tavern wench to be stared at. Give it to me, I say!"

Eldran shook his head. "Alone in the heart of the Kezankians, naked as a slave girl on the auction block, and still you demand and give orders. Take garments from the hillmen, if you wish, but do so quickly, for we must leave this place. There are others of their sort about. If you do not wish me to watch, I will not." Taking up his bow again, he nocked an arrow, and his eyes scanned the mountain slopes. "Hurry, girl."

Face flushed with anger and some other emotion she did not quite understand, Jondra refused even to look at the corpses. "Their garments are filthy and bloodstained," she said, biting off each word. "You must provide me decent garb. Such as your cloak!"

"Wiccana has cursed me," the Brythunian said as if she had not spoken, "that she made your eyes touch my soul. There are many women in my native land, but I must come to here, and see you. I look into your eyes, and I feel your eyes touch me, and there are no other women. It is you I want to bear my children. A petulant, pampered woman whose very blood is arrogance. Why should I so want a woman such as you? Yet my heart soars at the sight of you."

Jondra's mouth worked in soundless fury. Petulant! Bear his children! And he went on, saying unbearable things, things she did not want to hear. Her hand found a fist-sized rock by the water, and, with no more thought than white-hot rage, she hurled it. She gave a shocked gasp when Eldran crumpled bonelessly. A thin line of blood trickled down his temple.

"Eldran?" she whispered.

Frantically she crawled to his unmoving form, held a hand before his mouth. He still breathed. Relief filled her, stronger than she would have believed possible. She hesitated over touching the bloody gash where the stone had struck, then instead gently smoothed back his curling brown hair.

Suddenly her hand jerked back as if burned. What was she doing? She had to be gone before he regained consciousness. At best he would start his ranting again, about her bearing his children and the like. At worst. . . . She remembered the ease with which he had carried her—and firmly pushed away the memory of feeling protected while he did so. He was strong. Strong enough to force his will with her. She must go quickly.

The first of her needs was water, and she dropped down beside the pool to drink until she felt she would burst at one more swallow. The cool water invigorated her. Limping, she walked back to Eldran. He must be the source of what she needed. Truly she could not bring herself to touch the hillmen's garments, but things of his were another matter.

His bow she snatched up with an excited murmur, and raised it to test the pull. In astonishment she stared from the bow to the man on the ground. She had never met the man who could pull a stronger bow than she, but this bow she could not draw a handspan. Reluctantly she laid it on the ground beside him.

The sword she did not touch, for she had no skill with the weapon. Instead she slipped the tall Brythunian's dagger from his belt. Once she made slits in his fur-lined cape for her head and arms, it made a passable tunic, when belted with one of the rawhide thongs that had tied his fur leggings. The leggings themselves she cut to wrap around her feet, then tied with pieces of the other thong.

And then she was ready to go. For long moments she knelt by Eldran's side, hesitating. Some men never awoke from head injuries. What if he needed care?

"Jondra?" he murmured. Though his eyes remained closed, his hands reached out as if searching for her.

She started back from it as from a snake. He must care for himself, she decided.

At the start she kept her pace slow, for the mountainous terrain was rough at best. Her ankle would give no trouble if she did not overtax it, she thought. But after a time her thoughts drifted to Eldran, too. He had been near to waking when she left. He would be dazed, at first, but not too dazed to know she was gone, nor to remember what she had done. He was a hunter. Her hunters could track. There was no reason to suppose the Brythunian could not. And Eldran had two good legs on which to walk.

Almost without realizing it she began to press for speed. The ache in her ankle grew, but she ignored it. Eldran would be following her. She had to keep ahead of him. Her breath came in gulps. Her mouth was dry as if she had never drunk, and her throat as well. She was a hunter, too, she told herself. She knew how to watch for prey; she could also watch for a pursuer. Constantly she studied her backtrail, till she spent nearly as much time looking over her shoulder as looking ahead.

Rounding a thick, stone spire, she had taken three staggering, limping strides before she saw the half-score hillmen, sitting their horses and staring at her in amazement.

"A gift from the old gods!" one of them shouted, and booted his horse forward.

Jondra was too tired to struggle as he tangled a hand in her hair and pulled her belly-down across his mount before his saddle pad. Weeping in exhausted despair, she sagged unresisting as the hillman flipped up the tail of Eldran's cloak and fondled her bare buttocks.

"He will save me," she sobbed softly into the shaggy fur beneath her face. "He will save me." And a part of her mind wondered why the countenance she conjured was that of the Brythunian.

Chapter 19

Conan's teeth ground as he stared into the crevice where he had hidden Tamira. Staring, he knew, would do no good. She was not likely to appear from the mere force of his looking.

Forgetting the crack in the stone, he examined the ground and frowned. There was little that was enlightening. The ground was too stony to take footprints, but he had learned to track in the mountains of Cimmeria, and the ground in one set of mountains was not too unlike that in another. Here a rock was scraped. There another had its dark bottom turned up to the light. The story he found was perplexing. Tamira had left. That, and nothing more. He could find no sign that hillmen or anyone else had come to take her. She had simply gone. Nor had she waited long after his own departure to do so, for he could see remnants of the night's dew on some of the overturned stones.

"Fool wench," he growled. "Now I have two of

you to find.'' And when he found the thief, he vowed, he would wear out a switch.

Carrying his spear at the trail, Conan set out at a lope, easily following the scattered sign. As he did he felt like cursing. It was clear where she had headed. The camp. The rubies. Perhaps she finally had them, for he remembered the iron chests had not been in the ashes of Jondra's tent.

Suddenly he stopped, frowning at the rocky ground. There had been a struggle here, among several people. He picked up a torn scrap of white cloth. It was a piece of a servant's tunic, like the one Tamira had been wearing. He crumpled it in his fist.

''Fool wench,'' he said again, but softly.

Warily, now, he went on, eyes searching as much for hillmen as for signs of passage. After a time he became aware that he was following three tracks. Two were of men on horseback, one the set he followed, one much fresher. Newest of all were the tracks of several men afoot. Hillmen did not travel far without their shaggy horses, and there were not enough of them to be soldiers. He could think of no other group at large in the mountains, for if any of the Zamoran hunters remained alive they were certainly seeking the lowlands as fast as they could.

Suspicions roused, he looked even more carefully for likely ambush sites. The Kezankians had a wealth of such places, which did not make his task easier. Sharp bends around precipitous slopes and narrow passages between sheer walls were common. Yet it was a small valley bordered by gentle slopes that first halted him.

From the end of a deep ravine that opened into the valley, he studied it. Motionless, he stood close against the rock wall. It was motion which drew the eye more than anything else. Stunted trees dotted the slopes, but in numbers too small to provide cover. From the valley floor to the peaks there were few boulders or depressions to hide attackers, and those lay half-way to the summit on both sides. Hillmen liked to be close for their ambushes, to allow their prey little time to react. Everything his eyes could see told him the valley was safe, but instinct prickled in the back of his skull. Instinct, which had saved him more than once, won out.

Swiftly he retreated down the ravine. At a place where the wall had collapsed in a fan of rock, nearly blocking the way, he climbed up and out. Patient as a hunting cat he moved from boulder to boulder, twisted tree to twisted tree, following every fold and dip in the land.

Finally he found himself on the slope above the valley. Below him, crouched behind a jagged boulder with bow in hand, was a man. Conan grunted softly in surprise. Though he lacked fur leggings, the embroidered tunic marked the ambusher as a Brythunian. In fact, Conan knew him for the leader of those who had come to Jondra's camp in the hills. Frowning, he eased silently down the incline. Just above the watcher he stopped, settled his cloak about his shoulders and sat with his spear leaning against his shoulder.

"Whom do you wait for, Eldran of Brythunia?" he asked conversationally.

The Brythunian did not start. Instead he looked calmly over shoulder. "You, Conan of Cimmeria," he said. "Though I will admit I did not know it was you who followed us."

"Not you," Conan said. "Hillmen. And you can tell the rest of your men to come out. Unless you think they really have need to watch my back."

Grinning, Eldran sat up. "So we both know what we are about." He waved his arm, and one by one seven men in fur-leggings and embroidered tunics appeared on the slope, trotting to join them. "Do you, too, seek to rescue Jondra, then, Cimmerian?"

Conan drew a long breath. "So she is in the hands of the hillmen. Yes, I seek her, though it was another woman, also a captive, I first set out to find. But you speak as if you also wish to rescue Jondra. This puzzles me, considering the warmth of your last meeting with her."

"We have met since, she and I," Eldran said ruefully, "and there was even less warmth on her part. Some time after, I found where she had fallen captive to hillmen." He fingered his rough gray woolen cloak, dirty and torn; it was a hillman's cloak, Conan saw, stained and dirty. "There are matters I must discuss sharply with that woman."

One of the other Brythunians, a bony man with a pointed nose, spat. "I still say forget the woman. We came to slay the beast of fire, and we must do it if we all die. We have no time for foreign women."

Eldran did not reply, though his face tightened. Another of them murmured, "Peace, Frydan," and the bony man subsided, albeit with an ill grace.

"So you hunt the beast as Jondra did," Conan said. "She learned better after twenty of her hunters died, torn apart or burned alive. Only she, myself and one other survived that enounter, and we barely. I would see the thing dead, too, Brythunian, but there are easier ways to kill yourself."

"The Zamoran wench finds the beast," Frydan muttered disgustedly, "while we find only tracks. Mayhap we do need her."

Again Eldran ignored him. "Jondra hunted for a trophy," he said. "We hunt to avenge dead kin, and to prevent more deaths. Your steel could not prevail against the beast of fire, Conan, nor any mortal-wrought metal. But this," he laid a hand on the hilt of his broadsword, "was forged by mages for that very purpose."

The big Cimmerian eyed the weapon with sudden interest. Objects of sorcery were not beyond his experience. Betimes he could feel the aura of their power in his hands. If this weapon was indeed as Eldran said, then his debt to Telades could yet be repaid. "I would heft the weapon that could slay that creature," he said, but the gray-eyed Brythunian shook his head.

"Once it leaves my possession, Cimmerian, it will journey, Wiccana alone knows how, back to the place where it was given me, and I shall never regain it in this life. Such is the way of its ensorcelment."

"I understand," Conan said. Perhaps it was as the Brythunian said, and perhaps not, but did Eldran fall, he vowed, he would see that wherever the blade journeyed, it came first to his hand. One way or another, if he lived, the debt to Telades would be paid. "But before the beast, the women. Agreed?"

"Agreed," Eldran replied. "As our trails have converged, perhaps we will find both women together. Haral continued after the hillmen who have Jondra, and he will mark the way so we may follow quickly."

Conan got to his feet. "Then let us tarry no longer if we would save them before they are harmed." Yet as they filed down the slope his heart was grim. Women captives did not receive kind treatment from hillmen. Let them only have courage, he thought. Let them only survive till he could find them.

For the twentieth time Tamira examined her bonds, and for the twentieth time knew the futility of such study. Leather cuffs about her wrists and ankles were attached to stout chains fastened in the ceiling and floor of the windowless, stone-walled chamber, holding her rigidly spread-eagled in mid-air. The slender thief's sweat-slick nudity glistened in the light from bronze lamps. The air was chill; the sweat came from fear, fear more of something half-sensed in the room than of her captivity.

Jondra hung suspended as she was, facing her, and Tamira exchanged glances with the noblewoman. The taller woman's body also gleamed, every curve of breast and hip and thigh highlighted. Tamira hoped she also shared the other woman's calmness of face, though it was slightly spoiled by Jondra's constant wetting of her lips.

"I am the Lady Jondra of the House Perashanid of Zamora," Jondra said, her voice quaking. "A generous ransom will be paid for my safe return, and that of my serving woman. But we must be clothed and well-treated. Did you hear me? I will give our weight in gold!"

The crimson-robed man who labored at their feet, drawing a strange pattern on the floor with powders poured from small clay bowls, did not glance up. He gave no sign at all that he had heard, as he had given no sign since they were brought to him. He murmured constantly as he drew, words that Tamira could barely hear, and could not understand at all.

Tamira tried not to listen, but the steady drone bored into her ears. She clenched her teeth to keep them from chattering. Basrakan Imalla, the men who had thrown her at his feet had called him. She would have wept for her belief that a holy man would protect her, but she feared that if she began she might never stop.

"I am the Lady Jondra of the House. . . ." Jondra licked her lips nervously. Her head tossed as she attempted to jerk at her bonds; a quiver ran down the length of her, but no more. "I will give you twice our weight in gold." Her voice was fringed with panic, and the tone of panic grew with every word.

"Three times! Four! Any amount you wish! Anything! But whatever you intend, do not do it! Do not! Oh, Mitra protect me, do not!"

The beautiful noble sobbed and struggled wildly, and her fear sparked Tamira's own to flame. The thief knew now what she sensed in the chamber, what she had not allowed herself to even think of. Sorcery. The very walls reeked of sorcery. And something else, now that she let herself feel it. A malevolent hatred of women. Sobs wracked her, and tears streamed from beneath eyelids squeezed shut as if she could hide behind them.

"You are vessels of iniquity!" The harsh voice cut through Tamira's weeping. Unwillingly she looked. Basrakan stood stroking his forked beard, and his black eyes glittered despite at them. "All women of the cities are unclean vessels of lust. The old gods themselves will prove it on your bodies. Then I will chastise you of your vileness, that you may go to the ancient gods of these mountains in purity."

Shuddering, Tamira tore her eyes from him, and found herself looking down at the design he had drawn, an elongated diamond with concave sides. A short, black candle on one of the points flickered beneath her, another beneath Jondra. The configuration of lines within the diamond pulled at her gaze, drew it hypnotically. Her thoughts fragmented, became a maze, and unrecognizable images came into her mind, images that brought terror. Shrieking in the depths of her mind she tried to flee, to find a refuge, but all was chaos and horror.

Suddenly the maze itself shattered. Gasping, she found that she could look away from the diamond. The stern-faced Imalla had seated himself cross-legged at one end of the unholy pattern. He struck a small gong of burnished brass that stood by his side, and she realized it had been that sound which had released her from the maze. Again the gong sounded, and he began a new chant. Once more the gong chimed. And again. Again.

She told herself that she would not listen, but her bones seemed to vibrate with his words, with the reverberations of the brass. The air within the chamber grew chill; it thickened and stirred. Its caress on her body was palpable, like the feathery stroking of soft hands that touched her everywhere at once. And the heat, rising.

In disbelief she stared down at the candle beneath her. The flame stood firm, untroubled by the breezes she felt stirring, yet it could not possibly be the source of the waves of heat that seemed to rise from it. But the heat came, from somewhere, licking through her limbs, making her belly roll and heave, changing. She tried to shake her head, tried to deny the desire that curled and coiled within her. Dimly she heard a groan of negation from Jondra. Vaguely she saw the noblewoman, head thrown back, hips jerking uncontrollably, and she knew that she writhed as well.

Her lips parted; a moan was wrenched from her. "Conan!" With the tattered shreds of reason left to her, she recognized an answering cry from Jondra. "Eldran!" It would not stop. Her blood boiled.

With a crash the doors of the chamber flew open. Tamira gasped as if plunged into icy water; all sensation of desire fled from her in an instant. Weeping replaced it, tears for the uncleanness that seemed to cover her.

Basrakan leaped to his feet. "Do you desire death, Jbeil?" he snarled. "Do you desire to join Sharmal?"

The gaunt man in the door bowed deeply. "Forgiveness, Basrakan Imalla," he said hastily, "but it is the Eyes of the Fire."

Basrakan pulled him erect by fistfuls of black robe. "Speak, fool! What of the Eyes?"

"Sharmal claims that a woman brings the Eyes into the mountains. And he describes her." Jbeil flung a hand, pointing to Jondra.

Through her tears Tamira met the noblewoman's eyes, and got a confused stare and a shake of the head in return.

Basrakan's blood-red robes swirled as he spun. Tamira would have flinched from his gaze if she could. Before it had been malign. Now she could read in them skin being flayed, flesh stripped from bone. Her skin. Her flesh.

"Two camps of outsiders were destroyed this night past." The Imalla's voice was quiet, like the first brush of a knife against a throat. "This woman came from one of them, Jbeil. Find every scrap that was taken from that camp. Find the Eyes of Fire. Find them, Jbeil."

Jbeil ran from the chamber as if his own throat had felt that blade's caress.

Basrakan's eyes, like ebon stones, were locked on Jondra, but Tamira could not break her own gaze from them. As she stared helplessly, she found herself praying to every god she knew that whatever Basrakan sought was brought to him. Quickly.

Chapter 20

From the scant shelter of a sparse clump of twisted trees above the hillman village, Conan frowned at a two-story stone structure in its center. Armed men swarmed in hundreds about the score of crude stone huts, but it was the slate-roofed building that held his eyes. Around him lay the Brythunians, and they, too, watched.

"I have never heard of a dwelling like that among hillmen," Eldran said quietly. "For the Kezankians, it is a palace."

"I have never heard of so many hillmen in one place," Frydan said nervously. His eyes were not on the village, but on the surrounding mountains. Half a score camps were visible from where they lay, one close enough for the breeze to bring the sour smell of cooking and the shouts of men searching through the low tents. They had seen more clusters of the low, earth-colored tents in reaching their present vantage. "How many are there, Haral?"

"A score of thousands, perhaps." The plump Brythunian's voice was a study in casualness. "Perhaps more. Enough to go around, in any case." Frydan stared at him, then closed his eyes wearily.

Through a gap between mountains Conan caught sight of crude stone columns. "What is that?" he asked, pointing.

Haral shook his head. "I have done little looking about, Cimmerian. I saw the woman, Jondra, taken into that building below, and since I have watched, and waited for Eldran."

"Rescuing her will not be easy," Conan sighed. "Are you sure you did not see another woman captive?" Once more Haral shook his head, and the Cimmerian resumed his study of what lay below.

"It would take an army to go down there," Frydan protested. "Eldran, we did not come to die attempting to rescue a Zamoran wench. We seek the beast of fire, or do you forget? Let us be about it." Some of the other Brythunians murmured agreement.

"I will have her out of there," Eldran replied quietly, "or die in the trying."

An awkward silence hung over them for a moment, then Haral abruptly said, "There is an army in these mountains."

Frydan's mouth twisted sarcastically. "The Zamorans? I am sure they would come to help us if we only asked."

"Perhaps they would," Conan said with a smile, "if they were asked properly." The others looked at him doubtfully, obviously wondering if he made a joke, so he went on. "Their general is one Tenerses, I understand, a lover of glory and easy victories. He has been sent into the mountains to put down a gathering of the hill tribes. Well, here it is."

Even Haral was skeptical. "Unless this Tenerses is a fool, Cimmerian, he'll not attack here. Why, he'd be outnumbered four to one at the very least."

"That is true," Conan agreed. "But if he thought there were but a thousand or so hillmen, and they on the point of leaving before he could gain his victory. . . ." He grinned at the others, and slowly, as the idea caught hold, they grinned back. All save Fyrdan.

"The tribesmen would all rush to meet his attack," Eldran said, "giving us as good as a clear path to Jondra's prison. Perhaps your woman—Tamira?—is there as well. Both sets of tracks came to this village."

Conan's smile faded. He had stopped counting hillman camps when he reached twenty, but Tamira could be in any one of ten thousand dingy tents. He could do nothing save rescue Jondra and hope to find the slender thief after. It was a faint hope at the moment, but he had no more. "Who will go to lure Tenerses?" he said grimly.

"Fyrdan has a silver tongue," Eldran said, "when he wishes to use it so."

"We should be about our charge. It is what we came for," the bony man said stiffly.

Eldran put a hand on his shoulder. "I cannot leave this woman," he said quietly.

Frydan lay still for a moment, then sighed and sat up. "If I can steal one of the sheep these hill scum call a horse, I will reach the Zamorans in half a turn of the glass. A moment to snare this general with my tale and get his block-footed soldiers marching." He squinted at the sun, approaching its zenith. "The earliest I could get them here is mid-afternoon, Eldran. With luck."

"Wiccana will give you her luck, and guide your words," Eldran said.

Conan turned from the leavetaking among the Brythunians to resume his study of the stone building. "I will get you out," he vowed under his breath. "Both of you."

Pain had long since come and gone in Tamira's shoulders, wracked by her suspension. Even the numbness that replaced pain had faded into the background, leaving only fear. She did not have to look at Jondra to know the noblewoman's eyes were directed, as were hers, at Basrakan, the man who held their fate on the tip of his tongue. She could as soon have grown wings as taken her eyes from his dark presence.

The Imalla sat, now, on a low stool. Idly he stroked his forked beard and watched the two bound women with eyes as black as bottomless pits. For the first turn of the glass he had stalked the room, muttering dire threats and imprecations at those who moved slowly to obey him, to obey the will of the true gods, muttering about the Eyes of Fire. Twice so long he had sat quietly, and Tamira wished he would pace again, rant, anything but look at her. His eyes no longer glittered; they seemed devoid of life or even the barest shreds of humanity. In their depths she read tortures that did not even have names. That which called itself Tamira cowered in the furthest recesses of her mind in a vain attempt to escape that diabolic ebon gaze, but she could not look away.

At the doors came a scratching. It was like the slash of a knife in the dead silence. Tamira shuddered; Jondra whimpered and began to sob softly.

Basrakan's scarlet robes rippled as he rose fluidly. His voice was filled with preternatural calmness. "Bring the Eyes to me."

One door opened a crack, and Jbeil entered diffidently. "I have not your knowledge, Basrakan Imalla," the gaunt man said as if he dared not breathe, "but these fit the description my poor ears heard." The gems he extended in his hands gleamed in the lamp light.

Tamira's eyes widened. The black-robed man held Jondra's necklace and tiara.

Basrakan put out a hand; the jewelry was laid in his palm. From beneath his blood-red robes he produced a dagger. Almost delicately he picked at the settings around the two great rubies. Gold, sapphires and black opals he threw aside like trash. Slowly his hands rose before his face, each cupping one sanguine gem.

"They are mine at last," he said as if to himself.

"All power is mine." His head swiveled—no other muscle moved—to regard the two naked women suspended in chains. "Before this sun sets the doubters will have their proof. Confine these women, Jbeil. This day they will be given to the old gods."

Tamira shivered, and for an instant she teetered on the brink of unconsciousness. Given to the old gods. Sacrificed—it could mean no other. She wanted to cry out, to plead, but her tongue clove to the roof of her mouth. Wildly she stared at the swarthy, turbanned men who appeared to take her from her bonds. Her limbs would not work; she could not stand unaided. As she was carried from the room, her eyes sought desperately for Basrakan, the man who had the power of life and death here, the man who could, who must change his edict. The stern-faced Imalla stood before a table on which rested the rubies, his long fingers busy among vials and flasks.

The door closed, shutting off Tamira's view, and a wordless wail of despair rose in her throat. She tried to find moisture in her mouth so that she might beg the cold-eyed men who bore her unheeding of her nudity. To them she might as well not be a woman. Sacrificial meat, she shrieked in her mind.

Inexorably, she was carried on, down winding stone steps into musty corridors. A thick iron-bound door opened, and she was thrown to land heavily on hard-packed earth. With a hollow boom the door slammed.

Escape, she thought. She was a thief, a skilled

thief, used to getting into places designed to keep her out. Surely she could get out of one meant to keep her in. Awkwardly, for the stiffness of her arms and legs, she pushed up to her knees and surveyed her prison. The dirt floor, rough stone walls, the obdurate door. There was nothing else. Dim light filtered down from two narrow slits near the ceiling, twice the height of a tall man above her head. Her momentary burst of hope faded away.

A whimper reminded her that she was not alone. Jondra lay huddled on the dirt, her head in her arms. "He will never find me," the noblewoman wept bitterly.

"He will find us," Tamira said stoutly, "and save us." To her shock she realized that, though all her other hopes were gone, one still remained. She had never asked favor or aid from any man, but she knew with unshakeable certainty that Conan would find her. She clung to an image of him breaking down the heavy, iron-bound door and bearing her away, clutched at it the way a drowning man would clutch a raft.

Jondra did not stop her slow, inconsolable sobbing. "He does not know where I am. I hit him with a rock, and. . . . I do not want to die."

Tamira crawled to the taller woman and shook her by a shoulder. "If you give up, then you are dead already. Do you think I did not know terror to my soul in that chamber above?" She made a disgusted sound deep in her throat. "I've seen virgin girls on the slave block with more courage than you. All of that vaunted pride was camouflage for a sniveling worm ready to crawl on her belly.''

Jondra glared up at her with some spark of her old spirit, but there was still a plaintive note in her voice. ''I do not want to die.''

''Nor do I,'' Tamira replied, and abruptly the two women were clinging to each other, trembling with their fear yet drawing strength each from the other. ''You must say it,'' Tamira whispered fiercely. ''Say it, and believe it. *He will save us.*''

''He will save us,'' Jondra said hoarsely.

''*He will save us.*''

''He will save us.''

Basrakan intoned the last word, and his eyes opened wide with awe at the rush of strength through his veins. He felt as if a single bound would take him the length of the room. He drew a deep breath and thought he could detect each separate odor in the room, sharp and distinct. So this was what it was to be bonded with the drake.

On the table the glow faded from the rubies, from the lines of power drawn there in virgins' blood and powdered bone and substances too dreadful for mortal men to speak their names. But the glow that permeated Basrakan's very marrow did not fade. Triumph painted his face.

''We are one,'' he announced to the chamber, to the dangling chains where the women had hung. ''Our fates are one. It *will* obey my summons now.''

*   *   *

Tamira started as the door opened, crashing back against the stone wall. She felt Jondra tense as Basrakan appeared in the opening.

"It is time," the Imalla said.

"He will save us," Tamira whispered, and Jondra echoed, "He will save us."

"They are stirring," Eldran said.

Conan nodded, but did not take his eyes from the two-story stone structure below. From all the camps hillmen were moving, thick lines of them filing toward the stone columns that peeked through the gap between mountains. In the village five score turbanned men stood before the stone building. A red-robed man with a forked beard and multi-hued turban stepped out, and a muffled roar rose from the waiting hillmen, the words of it lost with the distance.

The Cimmerian stiffened as Jondra appeared, naked, arms bound behind her, a guard to either side with drawn tulwar. And behind her came Tamira, tied and bare as well.

"They are together," Eldran said excitedly. "And unharmed, so far as I can see. Alive, at least, praise Wiccana."

"So far," Conan said.

The skin between the Cimmerian's shoulderblades prickled. There was much about the scene below that did not please him, much beside the way the women were being treated. Where were they being taken, and why? Why?

The hundred hillmen formed a rough, hollow circle about the red-robed man and the two women. The procession joined the streams flowing toward the distant columns.

"This feels ill," Conan said. Unconsciously he eased his ancient broadsword in its worn shagreen sheath. "I do not think we can wait longer."

"Just a little longer," Haral pleaded. "Fyrdan will bring the soldiers soon. He will not fail."

"Not soon enough, it seems," Conan said. He got to his feet and dusted his hands together. "I think I will take a stroll among the hillmen."

With a grin, Eldran straightened. "I feel the need of stretching my legs as well, Cimmerian."

"You young fools!" Haral spluttered. "You'll get your heads split. You'll . . . you'll. . . ." With a growl he stood up beside them. "We'll need turbans, if we're to pass for hillmen long enough to keep our heads." The others were on their feet now, too.

"There is a camp just down the mountain," Conan said, "and none in it save women and children, that I can see."

"Then let us be about our walk," Eldran said.

"These old bones aren't up to this any more," Haral complained.

The small file of men started down the mountain.

". . . For the time of our glory has come," Basrakan cried to the throngs of turbanned men jammed shoulder to shoulder on the mountainsides about the amphitheater. Their answering roar washed over him. "The time of the old gods' triumph is upon us!" he called. "The sign of the true gods is with us!"

He spread his arms, and the flow of power through his bones made him think he might fly. Loudly he began to chant, the words echoing from the slopes. Never had so many seen the rite, he thought as the invocation rang out. After this day there would be no doubters.

His dark eyes flickered to the two naked women dangling from their wrists against the iron posts in the center of the circle of crude stone pillars. It was fitting, he thought, that those who brought him the Eyes of Fire should be the sacrifice now, when the new power that was in him was made manifest to his people. They struggled in the bonds, and one of them cried a name, but he did not hear. The glory of the old gods filled him.

The last syllable hung in the air, and vibration in the stone beneath his feet told Basrakan of the coming. He drew breath to announce the arrival of the sign of the true gods' favor.

From the masses on the slopes shouts and cries drifted, becoming louder. Basrakan's face became like granite. He would have those who dared disturb this moment flayed alive over a slow fire. He would. . . . There were men within the circle! Abruptly the words penetrated his mind.

"Soldiers!" was the cry. "We are attacked!"

*   *   *

Walking hunched to disguise his height, with his cloak drawn tightly around him, Conan pushed through the pack of hillmen quickly, giving no man more than an instant to see his face. Grumbles and curses followed him. A roughly wound turban topped his black mane, and his face was smeared with soot and grease from a cooking pot, but he was grateful that men saw what they thought they should see, no matter what their eyes told them. The wide circle of crude stone columns was only a few paces away. Conan kept his head down, but his eyes were locked on the two women. A few moments more, he thought.

A murmur ran through the crowd, growing louder. Far down the mountain someone shouted, and other voices took up the cry. It had been more than the big Cimmerian expected to go undetected so long. Best to move before the alarm became general. Grasping his sword hilt firmly, Conan tore off the turban and leaped for the circle of columns.

As he passed between two of the roughly hewn pillars he realized what words were being shouted. "Soldiers! We are attacked! Soldiers!" Over and over from a thousand throats. Fyrdan, he thought, laughing. They might live through this yet.

Then he was running across the uneven granite blocks, blade bared. The red-robed man, forked beard shaking with fury, shouted at him from atop a tunnel built of stone that seemed to reach back into the mountain, but Conan did not hear. Straight to the blackened iron posts he ran. Tears sprang into Tamira's eyes when she saw him.

"I knew you would come," she laughed and cried at the same time. "I knew you would come."

Swiftly Conan sawed apart the leather cords on her wrists. As she dropped, he caught her with an arm around her slim waist, and she tried to twine her arms about his neck.

"Not now, woman," he growled. In a trice he had her slender nudity bundled in his cloak. From the corner of his eye he saw that Eldran had treated Jondra the same. "Now to get out," he said.

Haral and the other Brythunians were within the columned circle, all facing outwards with swords in hand. From outside, bearded faces stared at them, some with disbelief, some with anger. And some, Conan saw in amazement, some with fear. Tulwar hilts were fingered, but none moved to cross the low granite wall atop which the columns stood.

From afar came the sounds of Zamoran drums beating furiously. The clash of steel drifted faintly in the air, and the shouts of fighting men.

"Mayhap we can just stay here till the soldiers come," Haral said unsteadily.

A ripple ran through the hillmen pressed against the circle's perimeter.

"Stay back!" the red-robed man cried. "The unbelievers will be dealt with by—"

Screaming at the top of their lungs, a score of turbanned warriors leaped into the circle with steel flashing against the Brythunians. By ones and twos, others joined them. Conan wished he knew what held the rest back, but there was suddenly no time for thought.

The Cimmerian blocked a tulwar slash aimed at his head, booted another attacker full in the belly. The second man fell beneath the feet of a third. The Cimmerian's steel pivoted around his first opponent's curved blade to drive through a leather-vested chest. He wanted to spare a glance for Tamira, but more hillmen were pressing on him. A mighty swing of his ancient broadsword sent a turbanned head rolling on the granite blocks, then continued on to rip out a bearded throat in a spray of blood.

Battle rage rose in him, the fiery blood that drowned reason. Hillmen rushed against him, and fell before a whirlwind of murderous steel. His eyes burned like azure flames, and all who looked into them knew they saw their own death. In some small corner of his mind sanity remained, enough to see Eldran, facing three hillmen and pushed almost to the low stone wall, fighting with broadsword in one hand and tulwar in the other. Haral and another Brythunian stood back to back, and a barricade of corpses slowed others who tried to reach them.

Abruptly the hillman who faced Conan backed away, dark eyes going wide with horror as he stared past the Cimmerian's shoulder. The tribesmen outside the circle were silent, pressing back from the stone columns. Conan risked a backward glance, and clamped his teeth on an oath.

Slowly the iridescent form of the beast of fire

moved from the stone tunnel, its great golden eyes coldly surveying the arena filled with men who slowed and ceased their struggles as they became aware of it. One of the leathery bulges on its back had split; the edge of what appeared to be a wing, like that of a great bat, protruded. And almost beneath its feet crouched Tamira and Jondra.

"Behold!" the red-robed mage cried, flinging wide his arms. "The sign of the true gods is with us!"

For an instant there was silence save for the dimly heard sounds of distant battle. Then Eldran shouted. "Cimmerian!" The Brythunian's arm drew back; the ancient broadsword with its strange, clawed quillons arced spinning through the air.

Conan shifted his own sword to his left hand, and his right went up to catch the hilt of the thrown blade.

As if his movement, or perhaps the sword, had drawn its eyes, the brightly scaled beast stepped toward the Cimmerian. Memory of their last encounter was strong in Conan, and as the spike-toothed maw opened he threw himself into a rolling tumble. Flame roared. The hillman he had faced screamed as beard, hair and filthy robes blazed.

Conan knew well the quickness of the beast. He came to his feet only to dive in a different direction, one that took him closer. Fire scorched the stone where he had stood. The glittering creature moved with the speed of a leopard, Conan like a hunting lion. With a mutter of hope that Eldran spoke truly about the weapon, the big Cimmerian struck. A shock, as of sparks traveling along his bones, went through him. And the blade sliced through one golden eye, opening a gaping wound down the side of the huge scaled head, a wound that dripped black ichor.

Atop the stone tunnel the red-robed man screamed shrilly and threw his hands to his face. The beast reared back its head and echoed the scream, the two sounds merging, ringing through the mountains.

Conan felt his marrow freezing as the cry lanced into him, turning his muscles to water. Anger flared in him. He would not wait so to die. Fury lent him strength. "Crom!" he roared. Rushing forward, he plunged the ensorceled weapon into the creature's chest.

With a jerk, the beast's movement tore the hilt from his hand. Onto its hind legs it rose, towering above them all. If its cry had been one of pain before, now it was a shriek of agony, a scream that made the very stones of the mountains shiver.

The red-robed man was down on his knees, one hand to his face, the other clutching his chest. His black eyes on the scaled form were pools of horror. "No!" he howled. "No!"

Slowly the monstrous shape toppled. The stones of the tunnel cracked at its fall. A damp, leathery wing emerged from the broken bulge on its back, quivered once and was still. From beneath the beast extended a corner of scarlet robe, rivulets of crimson blood and black ichor falling from it.

From the hillmen on the slopes a keening went up, an eery wail of despair. Suddenly the thousands of them broke into fear-ridden flight. Even now they tried to avoid the circle of columns, but their numbers were too great, their panic too strong. Those close to the low stone wall were forced over it, screaming denial, by the press of human flesh. The circle became a maelstrom, hundreds trampling each other in their eagerness to flee.

Like a rock Conan breasted the flood, his eyes searching desperately for Tamira and Jondra. The men streaming around him had no thought left but escape, no desire but to claw through the pack, grinding underfoot anyone who slowed them. No man raised a hand against the Cimmerian except to try to pull him from their path. None touched a weapon, or even seemed to see him with their terrified eyes. They would not stop to harm the women deliberately, but if either woman went down beneath those trampling feet. . . .

Eldran's height made him stand out as he waded through the shorter hillmen with Jondra in his arms. The Brythunian scrambled over the low stone wall and disappeared in the wash of dirty turbans.

Then Conan caught sight of the gold-edged black cloak, well beyond the circle, being borne around the mountain by the tide of flight. "Fool woman," he growled.

The clash of steel was closer, driving fear deeper into the hearts of men still trying to flee. There was no room to draw or swing a sword, but here and there daggers were out now, and hillman spilled hillman's blood to carve a way through to safety. With hammering fists and swordhilt, Conan hewed his own path through the mob, ruthless in his need to reach Tamira. Screaming men went down before his blows, and those who fell beneath the feet of that frenzied horde did not rise again.

The hillman village came into sight. Around the two-story stone building swarmed a hell of panting, desperate men dragging screaming black-swathed women with squalling babes in their arms and children clutching their long skirts. Here knots of men could break off from the seething mass to seek their camps. Others paused in flight to grab what they could from the stone huts. Bright steel flashed and reddened, and possessions changed hands thrice in the space of a breath.

Conan's sword and the breadth of his shoulders kept a space clear about him, but he barely even saw the men who slunk away from him like curs. He could no longer find Tamira among the now spreading streams of hillmen.

Abruptly the slender woman thief dashed from the stone structure that towered over the others in the village. She gasped and snugged the gold-edged black cloak tightly about her as Conan grabbed her arm.

"What in Mitra's name are you doing?" the Cimmerian demanded fiercely.

"My clothes," she began, and shrieked when he raised his sword.

Deftly Conan brought his blade over her head to run through a black-robed man who ran from the building with a dagger in his hand and murder in his eye. The hillman's multi-hued turban rolled from his head as he fell.

"I was just," Tamira began again, holding the cloak even more tightly, but she cut off with a squeal as Conan swung her over his shoulder.

"Fool, fool woman," he muttered, and with a wary eye for other hillmen with more than flight on their minds, he headed for the mountain heights.

Behind him, clangor rose as the Zamoran army topped the rise overlooking the village.

Epilogue

Leaning back against a boulder, Conan allowed himself a real smile for the first time in days. They were at the edge of the mountains, and in their journey they had seen no hillman who was not fleeing. Certainly there had been none interested in attacking outsiders.

". . . And when Tenerses realized how many hillmen he faced," Fyrdan was saying, "he began shouting for me and his torturer all in one breath."

"There was little fun where we were, either," Haral told him. "These old bones cannot take this adventuring any more."

Jondra and Tamira, still swathed in their borrowed cloaks, huddled close to a small fire with their heads together. They showed more interest in their own talk than that of the men.

"It was hard enough with the Zamorans," the bony man laughed. "I thought I would have my hide stripped off on the instant. Then that . . . that sound came." He shivered and pulled his cloak closer about him. "It turned men's bowels to water. The hillmen stood for only a moment after that, then broke."

"That was Conan," Eldran said from where he examined the two shaggy horses they had found wandering, saddled but riderless, in the mountains. There had been others that they could not catch. "He slew the beast of fire, and it . . . screamed."

"And the Zamoran gained his victory," Haral said, "and his glory. It will be years before the hill tribes so much as think of uniting again. He will be acclaimed a hero in Shadizar, while the Cimmerian gets nothing."

"Let Tenerses have his glory," Conan said. "We have our lives, and the beast is dead. What more can we ask?"

Eldran turned suddenly from the horses. "One more thing," he said sharply. "A matter of debt. Jondra!"

Jondra stiffened and looked over her shoulder at the tall Brythunian. Tamira rose swiftly, carefully holding the black cloak closed, and moved to Conan's side.

"I know of no debt I owe you." The gray-eyed noblewoman's voice was tight. "But I would speak with you about garments. How long am I to be forced to wear no more than this cloak? Surely you can find me *something* more."

"Garments are a part of your debt," Eldran told her. He ticked off items on his fingers. "One cloak lined with badger fur. One pair of wolf fur leggings.

And a good Nemedian dagger. I will not speak of a crack on the head. Since I see no chance of having them returned, I will have payment.''

Jondra sniffed. ''I will have their weight in gold sent to you from Shadizar.''

''Shadizar?'' Eldran laughed. ''I am a Brythunian. What do I care of gold in Shadizar?'' Abruptly he leaped, bearing the tall noblewoman to the ground. From his belt he produced long leather thongs like those used to tie leggings. ''If you cannot pay me,'' he said into her disbelieving face, ''then I will have you in payment.''

Conan rose to his feet, one hand going to his sword hilt, but Tamira laid both of her small hands atop his. ''Do nothing,'' she said softly.

The big Cimmerian frowned down at her. ''Do you hate her so?''

Tamira shook her head, smiling. ''You would have to be a woman to understand. Her choice is to return to being a wealthy outcast, scorned for her blood, or to be the captive of a man who loves her. And whom she loves, though she cannot bring herself to admit it. It is a choice any woman could make in an instant.''

Conan admitted to himself that Jondra did not seem to be struggling as hard as she might, though she almost made up for it with her tirade. ''You Brythunian oaf! Erlik blast your soul! Unhand me! I'll have your head for this! Derketo shrivel your manhood! I will see you flayed alive! Ouch! My ransom will be more wealth than you've ever seen if I am unharmed, Mitra curse you!''

Eldran straightened from her with a grin. She was a neat bundle in the cloak, now, snugly tied from shoulders to ankles with the leather thongs. "I would not take all the wealth of Zamora for you," he said. "Besides, a slave in Brythunia can have no interest in gold in Shadizar." He turned his back on her indignant gasp. "You understand, Cimmerian?"

Conan exchanged a glance with Tamira; she nodded. "I have had it explained to me," he answered. "But now it is time to take my leave."

"Wiccana watch over you, Cimmerian," Eldran said. Frydan and Haral echoed the farewell.

Conan swung into the saddle of one of the two horses. "Tamira?" he said, reaching down both hands. As he lifted her up behind him, her cloak became disarrayed, exposing soft curves and satin skin, and she had to press herself to his back to preserve her modesty.

"Be more careful," she complained.

The big Cimmerian only smiled, and spoke to the others. "Fare you well, and take a pull at the hellhorn for me if you get there before me."

As their shaggy mount carried them away from the small camp, Tamira said, "Truly you do not have to worry for her, Conan. I'll wager by the end of the year she has not only managed to make him free her, but that they are wed as well."

Conan only grunted, and watched for the first appearance of the lowlands through the gap ahead.

"It is a pity we must go back to Shadizar empty handed, is it not?"

Still Conan did not reply.

"No doubt some hillman has the rubies, now," Tamira sighed heavily. "You must understand, I do not hold it against you. I would like to see you once we return to Shadizar. Perhaps we could meet at the Red Lion."

"Perhaps we could." Delving into the pouch at his belt Conan drew out the two great rubies from Jondra's regalia. They seemed to glow with a crimson light on his calloused palm. "Perhaps I might spend some of what I receive for these on you." Tamira gasped; he felt her rumaging within the cloak, and smiled. "Did you think I would not know of the pouch sewn inside my own cloak?" he asked. "I may not have been raised as a thief, but I have some skill with my fingers."

A small fist pounded at his shoulder. "You said you would not steal from her," the slender thief yelped.

"And so I did not," he answered smoothly. "I stole them from you."

"But you would not steal from her because you slept with her, and you . . . I . . . we. . . ."

"But did *you* not say that should not trouble a thief?" he chuckled.

"Do not go to sleep," Tamira said direly. "Do not even close your eyes. Do you hear me, Cimmerian? You had better heed my words. Do you think I'll allow. . . ."

Conan tucked the rubies back into his pouch, then thoughtfully moved the pouch around on his belt where it would be harder for her to reach. He might not receive the triumphal parade that Tenerses would get, but his would not be a bad return to Shadizar. Laughing, he booted his horse into a gallop.

CONAN

☐	54238-X	CONAN THE DESTROYER	$2.95
	54239-8	Canada	$3.50
☐	54228-2	CONAN THE DEFENDER	$2.95
	54229-0	Canada	$3.50
☐	54225-8	CONAN THE INVINCIBLE	$2.95
	54226-6	Canada	$3.50
☐	54236-3	CONAN THE MAGNIFICENT	$2.95
	54237-1	Canada	$3.50
☐	54231-2	CONAN THE UNCONQUERED	$2.95
	54232-0	Canada	$3.50
☐	54246-0	CONAN THE VICTORIOUS	$2.95
	54247-9	Canada	$3.50
☐	54258-4	CONAN THE FEARLESS	$2.95
	54259-2	Canada	$3.95
☐	54256-8	CONAN THE RAIDER (trade)	$6.95
	54257-6	Canada	$8.95
☐	54250-9	CONAN THE RENEGADE	$2.95
	54251-7	Canada	$3.50
☐	54242-8	CONAN THE TRIUMPHANT	$2.95
	54243-6	Canada	$3.50
☐	54252-5	CONAN THE VALOROUS	$2.95
	54253-3	Canada	$3.95

Buy them at your local bookstore or use this handy coupon:
Clip and mail this page with your order

TOR BOOKS—Reader Service Dept.
49 W. 24 Street, 9th Floor, New York, NY 10010

Please send me the book(s) I have checked above. I am enclosing
$ _____ (please add $1.00 to cover postage and handling).
Send check or money order only—no cash or C.O.D.'s.

Mr./Mrs./Miss _____

Address _____

City _____ State/Zip _____

Please allow six weeks for delivery. Prices subject to change without notice.